LUCAS

THE EMBER TOWN SERIES

MJ JAMES

ebook ISBN: 978-1-958175-12-5

paperback ISBN: 978-1-958175-13-2

hardcover ISBN: 978-1-958175-14-9

To all my trans family. You are beautiful!

TRIGGER WARNING

As an author, I put a little bit of myself into everything I write. Before starting Lucas, I had to come to terms with the fact that I was not at a place where I could have top surgery. My own struggle turned into Lucas' struggle. Trans people are not "born into the wrong body," but we do have gender dysphoria. There are many reasons why we cannot medically transition, and I tried to write about this in a way that did not produce even more dysphoria. I personally found Lucas' acceptance of himself as therapeutic. However, as always, I will never have any hard feelings if you need to walk away from this story.

Lucas Contains
Body Dysmorphia
Deadnaming (censored)
Misgendering
Lack of Consent (for transformation)
Light physical actions on the page (i.e., kissing)
Off-screen physical relations

ALSO BY MJ JAMES

In-Between

The Immortal Part of Myself

NeurodiVeRse

Tonight, there were a dozen people in the bar in total. Enough to keep Lucas attentive but not enough to stop his brain from reminiscing. The music pulsed through the air, mingling with the laughter and conversations that echoed off the bar walls. It was steady for a Tuesday night. The bar was mostly regulars, faces that had become familiar to Lucas over the last two months.

With a sigh, he picked up a cloth and began washing down the unused part of the counter and open tables. In the corner was a group of slender women, all wearing short, spiky haircuts and jackets with their arms ripped off. They seemed to own that corner, the group always occupying the space even though the actual individuals changed. They didn't order much, just the infrequent sweet cocktail. Occasionally, they would flit around playing pool or darts, vibrating like hummingbirds, their movements so fast it was hard to tell if they were moving at all. They didn't cause any problems, and the owner seemed to have a soft spot for them.

At a table facing the door was another regular, Mika. She came dressed in flowing skirts and billowing shirts, almost like she belonged at a Renaissance festival. But her face was always somber, and her body was stiff, as if she sat expecting death to walk through the door. All that changed the few times another woman dared approach her and asked her to dance. The frown would disappear, and for a few minutes, her face would fill with peace. She would dance for the duration of the song, hanging on to the other woman like all was right in the world. Then the song would end, and she would go back to brooding.

Mika was the reason Lucas now stood behind the bar. On his first night in town, he had been staying at a nearby hotel when he had walked by and seen her dancing. He'd stood transfixed, watching the two women together with no one batting an eye. It had looked like safety.

When Lucas walked in, all eyes turned to him, an outsider in a place for regulars. But he'd moved toward the bar and ordered a drink. When the bartender, a big, hulking man, looked at his ID, he hadn't commented on the differences between the man sitting before him and the picture on the card. Instead, he'd just passed it back and asked what he was called.

Later in the night, after the bartender had gotten the idea of Lucas's story, he'd been offered a job. Lucas accepted immediately. Being caught between these walls made him feel at peace, as if his secret would be nothing if it had come out. Although he still kept it close.

It didn't take long before he was looking for another distraction, and he wandered back to the small kitchen to ask Rocko, the owner, if he needed help with anything.

Rocko was nearly seven feet tall and thick enough to have a hard time fitting through doorframes. His build was solid, although not precisely muscular, and he looked like he must have been some fighter who bought the bar after retiring. Although Lucas never asked. Asking about someone's past just gave them an invitation to ask about your own, and Lucas wanted that subject to remain closed.

"Do you need any help, Rocko?" Lucas asked.

Rocko gave him a glance, the kind that started at your head and went all the way to your toes, as if he had an X-ray that could see right through a person. "Not much more going on in here than out there. I'm good. Go mind the front. You never know when things are going to be interesting around here."

Lucas sighed as if he were a sullen teenager, not a forty-year-old man, and then returned to the bar. He took a second to compose himself and remind himself that changes in his body were expected, a second puberty, but it did not give him the right to act as if he were still an adolescent.

By the time the door opened, he had himself back under control. He glanced up, expecting to give the customer a friendly nod, and froze. It was a woman with light blonde hair that hung past her shoulders in wispy curls that looked effortless, but Lucas knew from experience that it took a lot of work to achieve that effect. Her lips were light pink and soft, and for a brief moment, Lucas imagined what they would feel like pressed against his own before he shook off that idea and tore his gaze away from her face.

She was tall, just short of six feet, with long legs accentuated by her tall black boots and a dark-blue dress that cut off mid-thigh. She was the most beautiful woman Lucas had ever seen. His mind filled with visions of his hands running up her milky white arms until they rested on her shoulders, mostly uncovered in the sleeveless dress. He looked back at her face, his gaze drawn to her crystal-blue eyes that stared at him hungrily.

Lucas broke away from the gaze, confused at the sudden lust that filled him. He had never before felt an attraction to a woman. He picked up a rag and began focusing on cleaning the spotless counters even as he felt her walking toward him.

She stopped right before him, letting out a deep, lyrical laugh that would fit any movie villain. "Don't worry, my darling." Her voice was as musical as her laughter, and as condescending. "Your appreciation of me does not need to send you into an existential crisis. It just means that you appreciate beauty."

"I ... um ..." Lucas stammered, at a loss for words. He cleared his throat and tried again. "Welcome to Rocko's. What can I get you? I haven't seen you here before. Let me know if you need a menu or the specials or anything." Then he shut his mouth before it started running away from him again.

Her eyes sparkled in amusement, then she turned and looked around the bar. "There doesn't seem to be much on the menu. Why don't you surprise me?"

Lucas nodded, afraid to open his mouth lest it betray him again. Then he reached down and started pulling up a bottle. This was his first bartending job, and he still got a thrill from putting together some of the basic cocktails. He stuck with a classic and made her a sidecar. It seemed to fit.

"Here you go." Lucas handed off the drink, intent on moving as far away as possible. The longer he was by her, the more uneasy he felt. Her whole persona spoke of a sweetness that was a vague camouflage for the venom that lay underneath. Lucas had been around enough toxic people and did not need to get caught up in any more of their webs, but before he could pull away, she spoke.

"I'm Veronica." She rested her fingers against her drink but did not make any motion to take a sip.

"Of course you are," Lucas said.

Her eyes widened at the comment, and her mouth quirked in amusement.

"I just mean that the name fits you quite well. You look like a Veronica."

"And you are?" she prompted.

Usually, Lucas loved giving his name. There was a euphoria to letting other people know who he was, one that only people who had gotten to choose their own names could feel. But he paused, hesitant to give out this simple information. Names didn't give people power over you, but their misuse of them could cause damage. Finally, he relented, manners catching up to him.

"I'm Lucas. If there is anything you need, just let me know." He tried to move away again, but she spoke before he could.

"I haven't seen you around. Ember isn't all that big of a town. I tend to know most people who stay here."

"I'm new. I've only been here a couple of months now." Lucas searched the bar, trying to find someone who needed him and would help him escape, but they all seemed to be avoiding him or trying not to get Veronica's attention.

"You're just passing through, a drifter trying to earn money before heading on your way." It wasn't spoken as a question but as a statement, as if she had already figured Lucas out and put him neatly into categories she understood.

"Nah, not passing through. I needed a change of pace and ended up here."

"You ended up here in Ember?" Her look became bewildered and then intrigued, and Lucas felt a flash of fear that he managed to make this woman more interested in him. "Do you have family from here?"

"My family is all back west. I needed some variety, and this seemed as good a town as any."

She took her drink and swirled it lightly as she looked at Lucas, but he took advantage of the pause in the conversation and, as if suddenly released, slipped away, putting as much distance between them as he could from behind the counter. Eventually, people began to resume activity, if cautiously, and Lucas started to focus on the other customers. He could almost manage to ignore the blonde woman who sat unmoving without touching her original drink.

It was only when Lucas went to hand Mika another beer that anyone even acknowledged Veronica's presence. Mika put her hand on his wrist, holding him at the table.

"Whatever you do, do not go home with that woman." Her eyes fluttered toward the bar as if she feared paying her too much attention.

"Don't worry, she isn't my type," Lucas said in an attempt at flippancy, but it came out weakly.

Mika looked at him in understanding but continued, "Remember that she isn't your type."

Then she turned her attention back to glaring at the door while sipping on her bottle of beer.

Lucas didn't know when Veronica finally left. He had been keeping an eye on her the entire time, but one minute, he turned his attention to a guest, and the next, the barstool was empty. He hadn't heard the familiar swing of the front door, so he kept watching for her, unsure if she had slipped into the restroom. As the night wore on, she never returned. Instead, her untouched cocktail was left on the bar as if a marker letting everyone know that she'd been there staking her claim. Lucas wasn't sure on what.

Lucas's body protested as he pulled himself off his mattress. He was too old to keep running on four hours of sleep, but any time he could get extra hours at the bar, he was going to take them.

He tugged on a pair of jeans so covered in paint splotches that you could no longer see the original color. He put on his binder, struggling to get it pulled down all the way. It was starting to stink. He would have to remember to wash it when he had enough time to let it dry. Next was his T-shirt, which had seen similar abuse, although you could still see bits of the black fabric under the spots of white paint.

His apartment was a studio above one of the stores in the downtown area. It was nothing more than a mattress on the floor, his clothing, and a few possessions thrown on shelves that once held inventory. And there was a small vase of red plastic flowers, the only thing giving the room any color. He had acquired them from a client's house after they had thrown them away.

He hoped to do more with his space. He wanted to turn it into a home, and he would, one day. For now, it was more important to save up all the money he could.

The alarm on his watch went off, reminding him that it was Wednesday morning. He pulled his testosterone off the shelf and took one of the needles out of the packaging. He plunged the needle into the bottle and pulled up, making sure to knock out any air bubbles. He was running out, and there were no more refills, which meant another visit to the clinic and another $250 to spend five minutes getting a new prescription. At this rate, it would take him over a year to fully fund the surgery that he needed. He couldn't cut back anymore. He already only ate his employee meal at the bar and whatever he could pick up at his other job.

When he plunged the needle into his stomach, he took a moment to let the stress melt away. Already, the medicine was helping. He been on it six months before he decided to start life over in Ember, where people only knew him as a slight man with no facial hair who looked younger than his forty years. He might not have a square jaw or a prominent Adam's apple, but more often than not, he was gendered correctly here. That was worth the unfurnished room and all the scrimping and saving. None of it would have been necessary if Rich had left him on the health insurance and pushed back the divorce just a little bit to allow him the surgery before they'd cut ties, but there was no point wishing for what had not happened.

Lucas fixed his binder one last time, ensuring it flattened everything, and strode out the door.

A yawn escaped him as he started his walk to his morning job. The company was run out of his boss's kitchen, and often, his wife had a pot of coffee going and would pour Lucas a cup without asking. He dreamed of a morning hit of caffeine to get him through the rest of the day. It would be enough to help him pull through the hours on his feet that awaited him.

It was a small painting company, just him and his boss, and Lucas had only been brought in because the owner's son had left to go to school. He would return in less than four years to start learning the business aspect and working alongside his father again. That was alright with Lucas; by then, the surgery would be complete, and he could go back to getting sleep. Or at least affording a few more meals.

By the time he reached the house, Matt, his boss, was already outside loading up the van, and the hope of coffee drifted away. Lucas tried to suppress another yawn as he slid into the truck's passenger seat, but failed. Thankfully, Matt's attention was elsewhere. It was going to be another long day.

"Where are we off to?" Lucas asked.

"Ms. Broadman called. She needs some more rooms painted."

"Again?"

In the few months Lucas had been working with Matt, they painted Ms. Broadman's house twice. Each time, the walls appeared covered in dark brown splotches that required several layers of primer to cover up the stains. Lucas only caught brief glimpses of her long white hair and hunched figure, which was at odds with the rumors he had heard. Apparently, she was a wealthy eccentric who liked to throw a lot of wild parties that left her house continually in need of repair.

The house was big enough to account for the rich part. It had a fence that opened to a driveway that required you to pull all the way up to reach the door. It had three wings sprouting off the entrance that were large enough to house the entire building Lucas lived in, store and all, or so he supposed. He had never been let into the main part of the house. Instead, they went in through a side entrance and were escorted to the wing reserved for guests. Once there, Lucas was not allowed to leave the room without an escort, even for a quick trip to the restroom. Matt didn't have the same restrictions and was allowed to wander around as he pleased, but he tended not to leave the rooms.

Lucas did not consider himself an exceptional painter, but he got the job done. Once they prepped both the rooms, the drudgery started. It did not take much concentration to dip the roller in paint and then coat the walls, and Lucas found himself slipping into a half-sleep as he worked. Occasionally, he would catch himself and try to focus more on the task until he drifted off again. Each time, he woke himself up, grateful that he had not fallen asleep in one of the paint containers.

In an attempt to stay awake, Lucas let his mind spiral off into a cycle of worry and regret that he usually avoided. There was nothing worse than reliving a past you cannot change, and he had spent too much time wondering why he told Rich at all. The truth had been struggling to burst out for more than a year at that point, and Lucas thought Rich would be fine with it. All the signs had been there.

One Friday night, they had sat on the couch, snuggling up with each other, watching the newest edition of a long-standing action series.

"All I'm saying is I get what people see in him," Rich said. "He is a fine male specimen. Given the chance, I would smash him for sure."

"Just him, or other guys too?" Lucas asked. He'd been pushing for the last few months, trying to look for hints that everything would be okay once Lucas told him.

"Sure, there are plenty of guys I'm attracted to. There is nothing weird about it. Sexuality is a spectrum and all that. But don't worry, you're still my favorite." He leaned his head down and kissed Lucas, whose brain was busy trying to determine if Rich was including him in the males he was willing to smash or if he was trying to convince him he still liked women. Lucas didn't think his husband was only into guys. He'd seen him look down at too many women's chests for that, but hearing him declare his attraction for men had given him hope. Lucas decided to press his luck as the words slipped from him.

"You'd still want to smash me if I was a guy?" Lucas tried for a teasing, seductive tone, but there was more than a hint of desperation in his voice.

"If you'd been born a dude, I would smash you." Rich leaned down, but Lucas spoke before their lips could meet.

"What if I already am one?" he asked.

Rich stopped and then pulled back slightly, staring at Lucas quizzically. It was the same look Rich gave every time he tried to determine if he should be upset about something. He was a big man who towered over Lucas at six-foot-five and had the frame of a linebacker. Even though Lucas was five-foot-seven, a respectable height for any gender, he felt small and helpless next to his husband, his now ex-husband.

"I'm just being silly," Lucas said. They had been married for twelve years, and he knew Rich well enough to realize that this conversation would not be decided in his favor, at least not this time. Lucas didn't want to risk losing him, not even at the risk of finding himself.

"This isn't something that you would joke about. Are you telling me that you think you are a man? You're one of those?"

Lucas felt his temper flare up at the statement. He might not have been willing to stand up for himself, but he found he couldn't ignore the hate being thrown out at every trans person.

"Those people?" he snapped. Then Lucas pulled away from Rich and stood in front of the couch. Even standing, he was barely on eye level with his husband, his now ex-husband, but his fury filled up the space in the room fast. "How did you go from being so liberated to being transphobic in the space of one conversation?"

"It's not the same thing," he said in the tone he used when trying to remain unprovoked. "You cannot just choose to change your gender. It doesn't make any sense."

Then Lucas did lose it, and the words came tumbling out.

"I didn't choose anything. I have worked my ass off trying to be your perfect wife for the last twelve years. I didn't choose to be a man any more than you did, but just because I don't have dangly bits between my legs doesn't mean that I am not one. I have tried so hard, but we both know. So, can you love me as a man?" He said this as a challenge because he already knew Rich's answer.

Except Rich didn't answer. He just stood, bumping Lucas aside as he moved upstairs. Lucas stood by, waiting for his husband to walk out the door with his packed bag, but when he came down, he handed Lucas the bag and a small pile of twenty-dollar bills.

"This should be enough for a hotel for the night," he said, then turned away.

"I'm not leaving," Lucas said. "You can't make me leave."

"The house is in my name," he said. "It's all in my name."

Lucas knew he should have fought harder, but nothing ended up being settled in his favor once the judge heard why they were divorcing. It didn't matter that he had dropped out of school to work three jobs to get Rich through his master's program with no student loans. All that mattered was that Lucas "defied the marriage contract," as the judge said.

When Lucas felt the tap on his shoulder, he lurched back, hitting the roller on his shirt, leaving another thick layer of paint. He looked around and realized they finished the last coat of paint. They cleaned the room, stashing everything in the back of the van, before driving back to Matt's house in silence. Lucas was always moody after he zoned out, and Matt was usually good at sensing it and leaving him alone when needed.

"We don't have anything tomorrow," Matt said once they reached his driveway. "Friday and Saturday, we have to repaint a duplex. Are you free?"

Matt always asked if he was free, as if he expected Lucas to turn and walk away one day. Lucas couldn't decide if Matt feared it or wished for it.

"Sounds good," Lucas said. "Same time?"

"Can you make it seven?"

"Sure thing."

Matt handed him the cash for the day's job, and Lucas walked off. He didn't know why Matt paid in cash and did so daily. It reinforced the feeling that Matt might have needed him, but that he would also be perfectly happy if Lucas didn't show up one day.

Lucas looked down at his watch. It was five-thirty, just enough time to head home and change, but not enough time for a shower before heading to his six o'clock shift at the bar.

CHAPTER
THREE

Rocko's opened at eleven in the morning, but Lucas never worked any of those shifts. The tips were horrible, and the bar was typically empty. Instead, he usually made it in around six and worked until two or three in the morning. If he didn't have his other gig the next day, Rocko let him stay until closing, which wasn't until six in the morning. Lucas had never heard of a bar being allowed to stay open so late, but Ember had some special provision that allowed it for accessibility reasons. It didn't make sense to Lucas, but he also wasn't going to complain.

Some nights, Rocko ushered him out the door long before his shift ended. The only explanation was that it was too dangerous for him to be there. It was typically nights that were quiet, where most of the patrons had left except for small, weird groups. Lucas protested the first time, telling Rocko that he appreciated being looked after, but he could hold his own. They both knew it was a lie. The testosterone might have helped his arms fill out, but it hadn't given him any sudden fighting skills. Lucas finally relented, deciding not to be around people who caused Rocko so much concern. It helped that the hourly pay still showed up on his paycheck.

Lucas was concerned that tonight would turn into one of those nights. It was quiet for a Wednesday. Usually, at least a few couples would be escaping for an early date night or some busi-ness people fleeing from one of the larger hotels a few blocks over. But for now, there were only the pixie-like women firmly entrenched in their section of the bar.

With nothing to do, Rocko gave Lucas the key to the small apartment above the bar. It was his home, but it did not give off homey vibes. The overall space was not very large, a studio with a shower and a toilet attached. There was a small kitchen area and a reading table. Except, every time that Lucas walked in, he couldn't help but feel that the entire place was staged. The bed looked like it hadn't been used, and the kitchen had never been cooked in. The shampoo and soap were always exactly where Lucas left them from the last time he used them. Lucas never asked Rocko about it, trying to respect his privacy the same way his own was being respected. Besides, he wasn't going to complain about the use of a shower, not after he felt so much better scrubbing the flecks of paint off of himself.

By the time Lucas walked back downstairs, the bar had started to pick up, and he stepped behind the counter, allowing Rocko to head back to the kitchen. Lucas felt a sense of joy fall over him as he made drinks, talked to people, and pretended to be good at all of it. It left him too busy for his mind to wander and get trapped in the past again.

He'd just gone from presenting a Liquid Sunshine to a young lady when he turned around and saw her … Veronica. He hadn't seen her enter; she just appeared. The couple that had been on the stool she now sat on were occupying a small table as far away as possible. He hadn't heard any of it.

Lucas tried to shake it off and moved to take her order. She was just a woman, not some mythological figure, and he had to remind himself of that.

"What can I get you, Veronica?" Lucas asked.

"You remember my name." Her lips curled up in delight.

"It's part of my job. You get better tips if you treat people like human beings."

With that, she laughed, a sound that cut through the rest of the chatter in the bar, and Lucas noticed a few startled glances when they realized where the sound was coming from.

"I think I would like wine tonight. Something red."

Lucas grabbed one of the open bottles of wine, the most expensive they had, and brought it over to her. She held the stem of the glass delicately between her fingers and brought it up to her nose to smell and then took the smallest of sips before setting it back down.

"Delightful." The words were more of a growl than a purr, but the seduction was intended either way.

"Well, enjoy," Lucas said, turning before she could say any more.

The night remained steady, and Lucas was able to make himself busy enough to stay as far enough away from Veronica as possible. He began to notice that he wasn't the only one avoiding the area where she sat. People chose to stand instead of taking the stools next to her or the tables behind her.

As the night began to wear on, she was still there.

"Lucas, oh Lucas. I think I need another." Her voice could be heard from the other side of the bar, and when he turned, the glass of red wine that she'd been nursing the entire night was now empty.

Lucas grabbed the bottle on the way over, hoping to spend as little time with her as possible. She might have a sweet exterior, but her interior gave monster-under-the-bed vibes. Lucas, of all people, knew that appearances were not always what they seemed.

"The same?" he asked.

"Yes, please."

As Lucas began to fill her glass, she started to talk.

"You said you have been here for a few months. You haven't stopped by before that?"

"No, I haven't," he said.

"Oh, sorry," she said with a simple laugh. "It is just that you seem familiar. I was trying to place you."

"Well, maybe we ran into each other the last time you were in California." Lucas realized that maybe it was too much information when he said it, but California was a big state, and what harm, really, could this woman be?

"Oh, no, that couldn't be it. I'm not a big fan of California. There's just too much sun. It has been ages since I have been back there. But you were born there?"

"Yes, born and raised. My whole family has been there for generations."

"That is just so interesting. It is so pleasant to know where your family is and where you come from."

Those words hit Lucas hard, and he turned so that Veronica could not see the pain that flashed on his face. He didn't know where his people came from, not really. It was just a long story of loss. First, his parents died, and then the family friend who had cared for him. When his ex-husband had left him, he'd been all alone.

"I think it is okay to be a little lost. No one can truly know themselves," Lucas said.

"Oh, I don't know. I think maybe we are the only ones that do know ourselves. It is making the world see you for who you are and accepting it; that is the hard part."

Her words froze Lucas where he stood. Something about the way she said them let him know that she knew exactly what it was like having to hide a part of yourself.

"Thank you for the drink, Lucas. Until we meet again."

Then she was gone, so gracefully that he barely noticed her move, and there under her untouched drink were several folded hundred-dollar bills. He picked them up and put them with the rest of his tips. He was that much closer to being able to afford the surgery that would help the whole world see who he really was.

It was close to four in the morning before Lucas left work. A bachelorette party had arrived, using the bar as their last stop on what had to have been a night full of copious amounts of alcohol. Eventually, when Rocko found Lucas asleep, clutching the handle of a mop in the middle of cleaning the newest round of upheaval, he'd been sent home. Lucas was so tired that he'd readily agreed and promised to be in early the next day to help with any lingering cleaning that would need to be done.

Lucas yawned, trying to wake himself up for the walk back to his apartment. The area outside the bar was well-lit to allow the riders to stumble into rideshares, and he took advantage of the space before wandering off to the darker streets. But it wasn't until the darkness enveloped him that he truly started to wake up. This was his favorite time of night, when everyone else was asleep in their beds. It was when he felt the most alive, the most alone, and the most connected to humanity.

His feet took him toward his apartment. He was so used to the walk that he didn't have to pay attention anymore. Instead, he let his mind drift to the mattress on his floor. It had already been a few years old when he inherited it, the springs a little too loose and pointy, but at the moment, Lucas couldn't imagine anything better than lying down on it.

A rustling sound brought him back to his senses. Lucas looked around at the nearest walkway, a small lane between two buildings filled with trash and discarded packaging, but he saw nothing.

"You're too tired," he mumbled. "Your mind's playing tricks on you."

Something cool clasped his forehead, pulling him back into a cold, firm body.

Lucas reacted instinctively, his years of self-defense classes kicking in. He flailed his foot back, aiming for genitals, and then went limp, hoping to startle the attacker into releasing their grip. Instead, the foot hit a solid bulk, causing his heel to hurt, and another hand reached out under his shoulder to keep him standing.

Then he heard the voice, the same one from earlier in the evening.

"There's no need for that," Veronica said. "You won't even remember a thing." Then she pushed his head to the side, exposing his neck. She moved her mouth, and Lucas had the sudden thought that he hoped she wasn't going to leave a hickey before he felt a sharp prick that turned into agonizing pain followed by the metallic smell of blood.

His mouth opened to scream, but Veronica's hand moved from his forehead to his lips, her hold a firm grip that held him securely.

She drank his blood, like a vampire in a bad movie. He knew that tonight he was going to die, and his last thought was that he hoped that they remembered to bury him in a suit.

Lucas woke up, his body on fire and his blanket drenched in sweat. He was lying on his mattress back in his house, the morning sun entering the window above his bed, except that wasn't right. Only his brain couldn't focus on that. It was too busy sorting out the pain that caused a spike to shoot through his body every time his heart beat. He screamed, or he thought he did; it was hard for him to know. Then he blacked out.

When he came to again, the sky in his window was dark and he knew that he was late for work. His mind fixated on getting up. Calling in sick wasn't an option; he needed the money. However, his muscles wouldn't lift him up to a sitting position, and it became apparent he could not go in. He at least needed to call, so he wasn't fired. He didn't have a phone; it seemed like a luxurious expense when he had no one who needed to get ahold of him, and for the first time, he regretted his decision. He was sure that Old Murray, his landlord, would allow him to use his store phone. Lucas just needed to stand up. He put his hand to his side, trying to roll himself the short distance between the mattress and the floor, but the pain was so intense that he blacked out again.

The passage of time became meaningless to Lucas. All that mattered was the pain. It flared through his veins like it was hitching a ride on his blood, traveling through his body. But slowly, ever so slowly, the pain started to lessen until Lucas was awake and conscious, staring at the ceiling.

Work, he thought, his first conscious thought since the pain had taken hold. He stood up. It hurt, but his limbs seemed surprisingly adaptable, like sleep had decreased his age by a few years. He ran down the steps, noticing the darkness of the night. He was late. When he got to the bar, he threw open the door, apologies leaving his lips before it even bothered to swing closed.

"I'm sorry. I wasn't feeling well; I must have overslept." Lucas went to walk behind the bar to take his place when Rocko stepped in front of him, barring his way.

"Son, look at yourself." His deep voice bored into Lucas, causing him to pause and take stock of the situation. Everyone in the bar, standing room only tonight, stared at him. He looked down and saw that he wore the same clothes he'd worn during his last shift. They were dripping wet with sweat, and he took a breath, breathing it all in. It was more than sweat. He stank like he shit and pissed his pants, and then slept in it. *How had he not noticed that?*

"I think we need to go outside to talk." Lucas went to walk through the kitchen towards the back door to the alley where the employees hung out, but Rocko blocked his way again and made him go back out through the front door.

"Where have you been, son?" Usually, when Rocko called him son, Lucas got a shot of joy that reverberated through his soul. Even though Rocko couldn't be much older than him, it was just nice to be seen for who he was. But today, he just felt embarrassed.

"I'm sorry. I got sick, and I couldn't call. I didn't mean to be late and didn't realize … how much I needed to shower first."

"What day do you think it is?"

The question threw him off. "Well, it's …" he started. "It's Thursday, right? Did I sleep through Thursday? Because I have a painting job on Friday, and if I miss that, I don't know if I'll still have that job." His mind filled with worry, but he found that he remained relatively composed. His heart didn't start racing, his breath didn't catch, and all the symptoms of his anxiety that flared up since the divorce were absent. *Huh, I must be getting a bit better,* he thought, before remembering his situation.

"It's Sunday night. Technically, it's Monday morning, nearly time for the sun to rise."

"Sunday," Lucas said. "How is it Sunday?" Lucas sat down on the edge of the sidewalk, and he realized that he really had soiled himself. "I don't know what happened. I was here … then I was in my bed and I didn't feel great … and now it's Sunday."

"It's okay, son. Why don't you go home, throw out those clothes, and get some sleep? You can come back tomorrow to make up some time. I'll call Matt and let him know what happened, but maybe you should take a few days off from the paint fumes."

He'd been sick for three days. The thought still didn't compute.

"Thank you," Lucas said before Rocko walked away, his arm covering his mouth and nose.

When Lucas arrived home, he found that his room was in a similar state as himself. He peeled off his clothes and washed himself thoroughly before throwing his clothing and bedding into a plastic bag. Then he spent the next hour scrubbing out his mattress, adding to its stained history.

Once that was done, he found that he could no longer sleep; the three-day slumber had left him with more energy than he knew what to do with, and he cleaned his whole house. It was small and mostly unused, so that didn't take much time. As the sun started to rise in the sky, he finally felt drowsy. He lay on the mattress and his spare sheet, but the sun seemed extraordinarily bright through his small window. Eventually, he took one of the trash bags, taped it up to block most of the rays, and fell asleep.

When he woke up, it was ten in the morning, an hour before the bar was set to open. He wanted to get in early to clock as many hours as possible. The time off had put a big dent in his timeline, but he knew if he worked hard, he could pull through, especially after the large tip from Veronica. At that thought, images began to flash through his mind. She was holding him in the street, biting his neck. He walked to the bathroom mirror and looked at himself. There was nothing there. He ran his hand over the spot; it felt sensitive, but that was probably just his imagination. A wound like that would not have healed on its own. It had to have been a fever dream. He'd sweat enough for one, that was for sure.

Lucas threw on a clean pair of jeans and his binder. They'd been scrubbed down and let out to dry earlier in the morning. Then he grabbed his button-down shirt with the alien head pattern. As he was about to leave, he turned back and grabbed his hoodie. It might have been the middle of summer, but there was something comforting about having a hoodie. When he went outside, he was glad he thought to bring it. The sun pounded into his head, almost as if he was walking around with a hangover, and he threw the hood up and sulked in the shadows of buildings until he made it to the bar.

Rocko opened the door when Lucas walked in, and if he was surprised to see the man there, he didn't show it. He slunk back to the kitchen, leaving Lucas to prep the bar and pour a few drinks for the pixie women who already claimed their section.

The first person to enter, besides the hive of women, was Mika. She sat in her customary seat and waited for Lucas to bring her regular afternoon order: a club sandwich and a coffee with a shot of Kahlua. The regulars had no need to order. He knew what they wanted when they walked through the door. It was one of the reasons he loved this job so much, and as he walked over the food to Mika, he was grateful that Rocko had not fired him. Most places would have the first night he didn't show.

"Rocko says you were sick." Mika didn't usually talk to Lucas. She preferred to sit and scowl until there was a pretty woman involved. He didn't take it personally.

"Yes, I must have caught something, and it wiped me out. I'm feeling better now."

She gave him a pointed gaze and then gestured to the hoodie he'd left on. The sun didn't penetrate the bar's stained-glass windows, but it still felt better having it on for now.

"I may not be as well as I thought, but I need to work."

"You're pale." It was a statement, not a question, so Lucas didn't bother answering. "You were out for three days?"

"Um … yes," Lucas said, uncertain if this questioning was concern or accusation. "I came in as soon as I could. My whole body hurt."

"Like fire flowing through your veins?" This was a question, so Lucas nodded in assent, uncertain how she knew. "Veronica was in here the night you got sick?"

"Yes, but I didn't do anything with her or go anywhere with her," Lucas spoke back a little too forcefully.

"What aren't you telling me?"

Lucas liked Mika, but the tone of this request felt a little too demanding. He contemplated walking away and returning to the bar, hoping Mika had conducted enough interrogation for the night. Instead, he found himself answering.

"I had a fever dream. I was walking home, and she stopped me, but I didn't see her. I remembered her voice; it was unmistakable. Then she sunk her teeth in me like a vampire and held my mouth shut so I couldn't scream when the pain started. But I was in bed when this happened, so it couldn't have been real."

Mika looked Lucas up and down and then swore under her breath. Lucas couldn't understand what she said, and it didn't sound English, but the meaning was unmistakable. She returned to her meal, scowling even more.

Once Mika finished her food and left, Lucas experienced a relief that he instantly felt guilty for. Then, he focused on the night. As it went on, Lucas found himself feeling better, as if he'd finally shaken off the sickness. The hoodie came off, and a new side of him came out. He felt young and free, and he twirled drinks with a flourish and spent a few extra minutes talking to people. Nothing life-changing, but it still felt good to be whole.

When a new party came in early in the morning, Rocko went to send Lucas home, took one look at him, mumbled under his breath, and then walked back out to the kitchen. Lucas stood confused but was grateful for the extra hours.

The group was a bit wild. They were an athletic bunch that seemed like they were together in the same way that the football team had hung together in high school. He could understand Rocko's concern, but the group didn't do much more than laugh and engage in pool and darts too competitively for Lucas's taste. However, at one point, Lucas could swear that one of the men pointed at him and said, "Looks like Rocko got himself a night-walker working here." But with everything that Lucas had been called in his time, a nightwalker seemed pretty tame, if confusing.

By the time Lucas's shift ended, the sun was appearing on the horizon, and Lucas was starting to feel the long shift drain on his reserves. He pulled his hoodie back on and threw up the hood before walking out the front door. He wanted nothing more than to take a nap before walking over to Matt's to ensure they were all good. The last thing he expected was to see Veronica outside the bar waiting for him.

"It's about time," she said. "I presume he kept you working all night as punishment."

She stood against the building across the road. It was a small bookstore that was firmly shut at this hour. Lucas planned to turn and walk away, but she was standing in the shade, and the sun had just started reaching over the one-story buildings and hitting directly where Lucas was standing. The sun felt draining and itchy, an emotion that he did not have time to process as the feeling of Veronica's teeth tearing open his neck flashed through his mind.

"Not now, please," Lucas said as he moved over to the shadows and proceeded to walk past her. "I need to go home and get some sleep. I haven't been feeling well."

"For three days, I heard."

"Why is everyone so obsessed with three days?" Lucas turned around and threw up his hands as he spoke.

"Three days is how long it takes most of the venom to make it through the system when a new vampire is turned."

"A vampire," Lucas said. He tried to brush it off, to pretend like it was all some sick joke that he wouldn't fall for, but he remembered his neck ripping and the feeling of death. As much as he tried to ignore it, it hadn't left him since that night.

"Surprise," Veronica said.

"I'm a vampire," Lucas said in a whisper. "I'm a vampire," he said again. The words came out slower, as if he was giving them shape, testing them on his tongue before sending them out into the world.

"Yes, yes, you're a vampire. Now, let's go before the sun comes out more." Veronica started walking, but Lucas stayed, watching her move away.

I should have known what she was, he thought as he observed her unnatural grace and the self-assurance that oozed off her. She was the embodiment of deadly, and he felt it from the moment he first met her, but there was no way he could have suspected that she was an actual vampire.

Lucas began to feel the sun's heat, even hidden in the shadows, and visions of exploding flashed in his head. Everything he knew came from movies, which never got things right. If he really was a vampire, he needed to get inside, so he turned opposite to Veronica and started walking back toward his apartment. He hadn't made it more than a few steps before the blonde stood in his way.

"Wow, how did you do that?"

"I'm a vampire," she said.

"Is that going to be the answer to every question I ask from here on out?"

She stood there looking at him as if he was a disobedient child, not the man she'd been flirting with a few days before.

Lucas tried to walk around her while still staying in the shadows, but every time he took a step, she was right there in his way.

"I'm not going anywhere with you," he said.

Veronica didn't respond. She just stood there, bored. As if to emphasize his helplessness, she held up her hand like she was examining her nails.

"In case you don't remember, you're the one claiming to have turned me into a vampire. I am not going anywhere with you. Who knows what you would do to me next."

She didn't move or respond, and Lucas felt rage boiling inside him. She'd turned him into a fucking vampire. He didn't even know what that meant, exactly. He just knew he needed a safe place to process the situation. But then it clicked in his head: he was a vampire. If Veronica could move fast, wouldn't that mean he could too? All he needed to do was get past her, and … well, he didn't know what to do next, but he would figure it out.

He sighed deeply, pretending to give in, and then tried to sense his muscles to figure out if they were different. Everything felt off. His best idea was to believe he could run super fast and that the rest would handle itself. When Veronica started walking again, Lucas took off toward his house. He willed his muscles to move like a track and field star, and he did go faster than his forty-year-old body would have usually gone, but it was nothing like the speed that Veronica had. She was back in front of him before he made it to the end of the business. Her hand clamped onto his shoulder, causing him to stop.

"Fine," she said. "We will talk, but not out in the sun." She looked around the street until she found a coffee house open for the early morning customers. Then she started walking toward it without looking back at Lucas.

He thought about running again, but he knew that whatever

made Veronica fast, he either didn't have it or didn't know how to use it. At least the cafe was neutral territory in front of witnesses.

They walked in together, Veronica holding open the door for Lucas, as if making sure that he did not make one last futile attempt to escape. The coffee shop was cute, with tables and comfortable chairs that invited patrons to stay. There was even a sign on the wall with the Wi-Fi password. It wasn't crowded, although a few people were sitting at the tables, and someone was ordering at the counter.

The barista, a slender woman in her thirties, turned to greet them and paled at the sight. The cup in her hand started shaking, and some of the coffee spilled from the sipping hole in the lid.

"Don't mind us," Veronica said. "We will sit over here in the corner. You can charge us for the coffee, but it is unnecessary to bring it over. If you wouldn't mind, you can close the blinds. This place is a little too sunny for my taste."

The woman didn't bother replying. She just handed the coffee cup off to the waiting woman and went to pull down the blinds—most of the tables emptied as well. Only one stayed, a male that Lucas recognized from the party the night before. He eyed them wearily as he continued to sip on his drink.

"People know who you are," he said. It also explained their reaction to her at the bar.

"Not everyone. There are humans here blissfully unaware that their city is a paranormal refuge. Although some know. The human who owns this place is a carrier. She has a few distant relatives among our flock, but none that have chosen to be changed in a few generations. Although, I have no idea why she is so scared. She knows she is off-limits. No matter how rich her blood, I cannot partake of it."

Lucas's mind spun, trying to make sense of Veronica's words. "Um, carrier?" he asked.

"Despite what television may have told you, not everyone can become a vampire. It is a genetic mutation. I don't know the details because I don't care. Others back at the ranch know; you can ask them more, if you please." As Veronica spoke, she scanned the room as if looking for someone who would challenge her or maybe someone she could challenge. But there was only that one customer who sat facing an empty cup, not bothering to hide that he was listening. The cafe owner had disappeared.

"This genetic mutation does not activate until it has a catalyst. We are the catalyst. Biting them activates some mutation, and they transform into one of us. It is a part of the kin, but we are not allowed to grant them the mercy of eternal life unless they ask, all thanks to the pathetic treat. They live and die as if they are mortals." This last was spoken louder, as if she hoped the human woman would hear.

"Then how did I … how am I here? I didn't ask for this."

"I don't know. Most of the kin live here. Those who choose to move away are known. You are not kin; I checked before being allowed to feed, yet here you are."

She said it so flippantly, like this change meant nothing, even though so many others had chosen to reject this life. *What happened to me?*

"Is there a way to turn me back?" he asked, the reality of his situation finally starting to sink in.

"Back? Why would you want to go back to that? You have been given a gift, whether it was meant or not. You are now one of the horde. You are now family. Who you are has been altered on a genetic level. There is no going back."

The more she spoke, the more Lucas felt as if he was being drafted into a cult.

"Well, I appreciate you telling me what has happened. I will go back to my house and think about this. After work tomorrow, maybe we can meet up again, and you can teach me more about what all this means."

She laughed then, loud and unrestrained, the musical tone filling the entire cafe. He half expected to wet himself in fear, but he wasn't sure that was possible anymore. There was so much that he needed to know, but Veronica was the last person, well, vampire, he wanted to learn it from.

"You cannot go back to any part of your life. You must stay at the ranch until you have been deemed stable enough to be left to your own devices. Then maybe you will be allowed more freedom, but it would take an entire council convening to do so." She turned in her seat and hissed at the man in the corner. "They say that we are dangerous, even though their young are allowed to mingle and even attend school."

The man stood up, pushing the table away from him. He said nothing, but his stance showed he was eager to engage if she pushed him. Lucas looked between the two, not understanding the tension.

"We must go," Veronica said.

"I can't. I have to keep working. I need money for medicine and surgery. If you take that away ... I'll go back. I can't go back to that." There was a desperate plea in his voice.

All the fight disappeared from Veronica, and a look of pity washed over her face. She sat back down, completely ignoring the other man.

"You can't."

"I have to. I won't hurt anyone, I promise. I need to keep working."

"No, you don't understand." Lucas had never heard her voice as gentle as it was at that moment. "You can't change. Who you are was locked into your genetic code when you were transformed. You can no longer change. If you cut your hair, your body will repair it back to what it is now, what it sees as right. If you damage yourself or remove parts of your body, they will grow back. You will never need to take hormones again, but you will also never change from who you are physically right now."

As she spoke, tears began to spill from Lucas's eyes. "No," he said. "No, no, no, NO, NO." Then he turned over and looked at the man, who gave him a slight sympathetic nod, and he knew that she was telling the truth. He ran his hands over his face and then his chest. With tears running down his face, he stood up, walked out of the cafe, and started to run.

Lucas knew Veronica was behind him, somewhere. He was not running fast, just desperately trying to leave all the pain behind because he'd given up everything to scrimp and save so he would finally have the body he was meant to have. Lucas had been looking forward to the little things, like the first time he could walk outside without a shirt. Or not having to wear a binder all day.

It wasn't that he hated who he was. He just wanted to live the last half of his life with the freedom to be himself. Now, he was faced with more years than he knew but in a body that would never change. So he kept running.

It was short-lived. The shade of the buildings began to disappear, and the sun filled the sky. He didn't explode, but his skin did start to redden and then blister. He found a tree and sat sheltered beneath its branches.

Within seconds, Veronica was beside him. "I called the main house. They will send a bus to come and pick us up."

"You called?"

"Yes, with my cell phone. We may be vampires, but we are not barbaric. We have electricity and plumbing, even though we don't need that as much. There are TVs, phones, and all the modern marvels. What did you think it was going to be like?"

"I don't know. Most cults have community gardens and spiritual services. Do we even have to eat?"

"No, we don't need food. And we're not a cult. We are a horde or a family. We have learned over the years that it is best to stay together until our young have the control to be on their own. But even then, you will not be confined to a room, deprived of modern life. I know this isn't what you expected, and I am sorry that it happened without warning. It shouldn't have, and I will figure out why it did. But you are one of us now, and we will ensure you are cared for better than you were doing on your own."

"I was doing just fine on my own," Lucas said.

Veronica rolled her eyes, and before Lucas could come up with anything else in his defense, a van pulled up. It was navy blue with windows tinted so dark that you could not see through them. The side door slid open on its own, and instead of opening into the vehicle, there were sun-blocking curtains hanging. Veronica took off at a run, making the distance between the tree and the road nearly instantaneous. Thankfully, it wasn't far because the sun was now high in the sky and barreled down on Lucas as he sprinted. It was an agonizing second before he was behind the safety of the curtains. Then, the door started closing on its own.

The van had three rows, a long row in the back and two rows of bucket seats. Veronica moved into the front passenger seat, leaving Lucas alone in the middle. In the front was a driver. He was dressed in a nice button-down shirt and a pair of khaki pants that seemed to hang on his legs even while he was sitting. The man turned and looked Lucas up and down. Lucas's heart stopped. He was caught in the deep brown eyes and the easy grin shot his way until he realized his heart had literally stopped. He threw his hands to his neck, checking for a pulse, and then his wrists. There was nothing. Even the veins in his arms seemed sunken.

"He needs to feed," the man said. "Has he had his first meal yet?"

"No, there hasn't been time."

"There is some in the emergency freezer."

Veronica turned around in her chair and gave Lucas a long look. "Are you hungry?"

Lucas just stared at her. Hadn't she just told them that they didn't need to eat?

"He is fine." Veronica turned back around, ignoring him again. "I think it will go over better if he feeds back at the Ranch."

"Then I suppose I should start driving."

Despite his conversation with Veronica, Lucas still expected to see a commune when they pulled into the Ranch. He didn't expect to see a gated community. The van stopped at a gate built of black metal that was no more than ten feet tall. Lucas couldn't help wondering if it was meant to keep vampires in or humans out. Maybe it was just a false sense of security for everyone involved.

As they drove in, they passed rows of suburban-like houses. Each was two stories and identical. The lawns were all perfectly manicured, the hedges uniformly lined on each side, with no deviation from the other. The driveways all stood empty, not a car in sight. It gave off dystopian vibes.

As they drove further into the area, the houses changed. They grew older, and there were signs of life. People were outside doing yard work, a few cars drove down streets, and occasionally, a human was out for a walk. Lucas assumed they were human since they showed no discomfort in the sun.

"You allow humans around?" Lucas asked.

"This is a haven for all kin. Those who choose to can live in the houses by the gate. These are home to our kind, the Changed. These humans are kin employed by the Changed."

"I will get one of these houses to live in?" Lucas said.

"Perhaps in a century or two. You are still young, and youth requires supervision. You will be staying in the Ranch."

The van turned from the older houses to a large driveway, like one that belonged to a mansion more than a ranch. The grounds, like the rest of the area, were well-manicured. It wasn't until they reached closer to the house that Lucas realized that the windows were all completely covered in black, allowing no sunlight to enter inside.

The van drove past the front entrance down a path to the side of the house that led to a garage. It was large, easily holding a dozen similar vans, plus some flashier cars that were not tinted, for what Lucas assumed would be night driving.

"This is the Ranch?" Lucas asked.

Veronica didn't bother answering. She and the man left the van and started walking to a door at the far side of the garage. Resigned, Lucas followed them. The door led to a hallway that seemed built to allow the travel between the house and the garage without concern over the sun. The open door on the far side led to a kitchen, if one could call it that. It looked like it would have fit well into a large restaurant. There were multiple fridges and stoves, all sitting pristine and unused. The pair walked through the room without a second glance. They trotted through an attached dining room with a table that could easily hold two dozen people with the same disregard. It wasn't until they hit the lobby that they stopped. It reached several stories, hosting a large chandelier that reflected light everywhere. The entire building seemed well-lit for a room that did not receive any sunlight. *The electricity bill must be outrageous*, Lucas thought before realizing that none of that was his concern anymore. It made him feel hollow and lost in the enormity of the space.

"Come with me." Veronica started moving before Lucas could fully take everything in. "It's time for your first feed."

Veronica walked down a side passage hidden behind the grand staircase. The hallway was lit by lights built into the ceiling, but the space was tight and dark.

Lucas shivered involuntarily, afraid of what waited at the end of the hall. He thought back to the horror movies he had watched, and his mind filled with visions of humans locked in cages; captured and destined to spend their days feeding the clan until their eventual death released them from their misery. He wasn't going to be a part of any of it. Instead, he would refuse and help the humans escape. Lucas would do anything to save them from the monster he had become.

This realization allowed his feet to keep moving, one in front of the other.

When they hit a set of stairs, ones built of stone that seemed older than the building, he kept going. When they reached the bottom of the stairs, Veronica typed in a code to open the door. Lucas took in everything, trying to build a plan on how to go about the big escape.

When they walked in and saw nothing, he stopped, uncertain how to proceed.

It wasn't nothing, exactly. It just was not what he had framed inside his head. There were no cages and no humans. Instead, doctors or scientists were walking around in white lab coats. There were microscopes on shiny silver tables, and off to the side, there were chairs with curtains that could be pulled for privacy, not unlike an emergency room.

One of the doctors, with short brown hair, a rounded face, and a collared shirt under the lab coat, walked up to them. They held a clipboard in their hands. "We have no more feedings scheduled for today," they said. Then they gave Lucas a second glance and looked at their paperwork in confusion.

"He is new," Veronica said.

"There wasn't a scheduled conversion," the doctor said, flipping more frantically through the papers on their board.

"He was unplanned."

The doctor looked up, the clipboard forgotten. Their mouth hung slightly open, the shock apparent on their face. "Does she know?"

"Unfortunately, yes. He needs to feed. His heart has stopped."

The doctor became professional, putting aside all emotions to get the job done. "He can go to room one. If you are his sponsor, you can join him." Then they turned and addressed Lucas. "Warm or cold?"

He stared at Veronica, uncertain what they meant.

"Do you want your blood warm or cold?" they asked again.

"It's his first feeding," Veronica said.

"Right, warm then." The doctor moved off toward the back of the lab.

Veronica walked toward the curtained space. Lucas turned around and headed back to the door they'd just entered. It refused to open when he turned the handle.

"I won't do it," Lucas screamed. "I am not going to make someone else suffer for my existence. I might as well walk into the sun now."

Veronica let out a loud sigh. Lucas felt her arms pulling him away from the door until he faced her. Everyone in the lab was looking at them now.

"No one is suffering for your existence. This is not the 1600s, and we are not barbarians. You should know all this already. Come." She did not give Lucas much of a choice as she held on to his arms and dragged him to where the doctor had gone. They walked into a giant refrigerator that was filled with bags of blood, all hanging, labeled, and organized on rows of hooks. When they entered, the doctor was selecting one of the bags of blood off of a hook.

"We are the largest sponsor of blood banks around the world. The blood is donated and perfectly safe," Veronica said.

"Then all this should go to hospitals to save lives."

"Most of it does," the doctor said. "This is blood that was donated specifically for biomedical research. We only take a fraction of it, just enough for us vampires to survive. Each family gets what they need. It is carefully tracked and monitored. Only older vampires are allowed to feed from a live victim. Usually, that is because they have formed blood relationships. One is never allowed to feed without permission. This way, no one is accidentally turned, and we stay safe from human retaliation."

"I had permission," Veronica said. "I waited days for the paperwork to clear before they said I could feed. This shouldn't have happened."

"They gave you permission to feed on me." Lucas turned to Veronica in disbelief. "What right did they have to give you permission to take from my body without asking me?"

"They rarely let us," Veronica said. "It's like they have forgotten the need to hunt to survive. They are so concerned with our image. It is just a bit of blood to sustain us, and the person goes on none the wiser."

Lucas pulled his arm from her grasp, and even though he knew she was letting him go, it was still satisfying. He turned to face the doctor. "No one was harmed?"

"No one. Everything is recorded and voluntary. Blood that makes its way to us has all been financially compensated for. Anything given without cost goes to hospitals and clinics."

Lucas nodded and turned to walk away but stopped at the doorway. "People in power have used the same excuse to control other people's bodies. They use it to justify a lack of consent, refusing abortion, and transgender care. They feel they should have more say over someone's body than the person it belongs to. What you did was no less a violation. You do not need to accompany me into that room. I will do this on my own. Afterward, I would like to talk to whomever I need to about getting a new sponsor. One that I choose instead of one who chose for me."

Then he trudged out, leaving the bags of blood behind. They were making him unsettlingly hungry. Lucas walked to the room, slid closed the curtain, and sat in the chair, waiting.

It wasn't long before the doctor brought in a large coffee mug full of red liquid. They put it on a stand at the side of the room and wheeled it until it was in front of Lucas, almost like a TV tray. Then they left as quickly as they had come.

Lucas looked at the liquid. He took in a whiff of its scent, expecting to be overcome with hunger and desire. Instead, it smelled like blood—metallic—and his stomach wrestled between hunger and revulsion.

He put his hands around the cup. As promised, it was warm, just enough that it didn't burn. Lucas put the cup to his lips, took a tentative sip, and immediately spit it back out. The blood sprayed the tray with watered-down red droplets.

"It gets better." The man from the van slid in through the curtain. "You still have some human parts to you. They will disappear more and more until the blood is no longer repulsive. It will never quite replace the flavor of a well-cooked meal, but you will find dining preferences. It is almost like wine that way, although the less aged, the better."

Lucas looked up at the man, uncertain what he wanted and if he should trust him.

"No one should have to do this alone. You are right. Hunting should be completely abolished. I have been advocating for it for years. The council is old and set in its ways. They do not always care for others' viewpoints if it inconveniences them. You will be the reason they agree. I will need your support to help me end this barbaric practice."

Lucas looked him up and down. The man was gorgeous in a carefree way. He looked to be in his mid-thirties, with dirty brown hair combed to the side, a chiseled jaw, and a sharp nose. "At least you are honest about what you want to use me for."

"Oh, I'm sure I could find a few uses for you. But not now. You're too new. There's still too much happening. So, yes, I need you for the council, but I also want to volunteer to be your sponsor. To help you understand the world that you have joined."

The hot vampire was flirting with him. Lucas could barely process the last part of what was said; his mind was too busy wondering what he would look like without a shirt. Eventually, the rest of the words caught up to him. He cleared his throat in embarrassment. "You're friends with Veronica?" It came out as an accusation.

"Do you know how many vampires there are in our family?"

Lucas shook his head in dissent, uncertain where this was going.

"There are only 150 of us. No one has decided to cross over since the last generation."

"Is what we are that horrible?"

The man shrugged and leaned against the wall. "Some desire to have children and then decide they can't leave them. Others get stuck on the idea of making themselves perfect before they change, but there is no such thing as perfection, and they end up in a loop until they realize they have aged. You cannot turn back time. So they give in and die. Others have no desire to be who we are. There is no sparkling when stepping in sunlight, only burning and blood. Would you have chosen to change if given a choice?"

Lucas looked down at his body; the binder was still tight around his chest, reminding him he would be stuck in this transition forever. "No." The word came out quietly, but it filled up the room.

"You need to drink. It is best not to think about it. Close your eyes and plug your nose if you must. It is best to do it all in one go and get it over with."

"What happens if I don't drink? Will I die?"

"No. You will become so overrun with hunger that you start attacking anything with a pulse. You become dangerous, and we cannot let that happen. So if you refuse to drink, then we will have to force-feed you to keep the humans safe."

Lucas gave a slight nod in understanding. He plugged his nose with his right hand and picked up the mug with his left. Then he closed his eyes and drank it down as fast as possible. It was still warm enough that he didn't taste it until it reached his stomach. Then, the metallic aftertaste left him gagging for a moment before everything settled. He had managed it, after all.

O nce the blood hit his system, Lucas started to feel more alive. His skin kept the grayer shade it'd begun to acquire, and his eyes still looked slightly hollow, like he'd not slept in days. With the fresh blood in his system and his heart once again pumping, he wanted to move.

After his feeding, he was escorted into a room by the sexy vampire who'd finally given his name as Jeffery. The room was on one of the upper floors of the residence, and it was an apartment all on its own. There was a living area, a bathroom, a large bedroom, and even a small kitchenette. Lucas found it ironic that most of the space was taken up by areas that he no longer had a use for. While he was still admiring his new accommodations, Jeffery backed out of the room.

"I'll be back," he said so quietly that Lucas was surprised he could hear the words over the key turning in the lock.

Lucas went to the door and tried the handle but was unsurprised when it held firm. He walked to the boarded-up windows and found they were sealed shut with a piece of metal securely bolted into the walls. Lucas was stuck, but there were worse places he could be.

Full of energy, he began to look closer at his new space. The kitchen cupboards were bare, not even dishes. The bathroom was fully functional, and Lucas figured that he would need to shower at some point. Even if he no longer perspired, he would still get dirty. To his amusement, the toilet was functional as well, and Lucas tried to determine what possible use there was for that, but then the memory of the doctor talking about volunteer blood donors came back to him, and Lucas decided that maybe these rooms were not always as free of humans as one would think.

The clothes in the closet seemed to have been selected specifically for Lucas. There were modern jeans and T-shirts like he typically wore. There were also brand-new packages of boxers in his preferred brand and a few new binders in his size. They'd matched everything perfectly, and it mostly made sense when he saw a bag on the bed containing his few possessions.

Lucas held up one of the binders and sunk to the floor with it in his hands. He wanted to cry, and he tried, but the tears wouldn't come. He knew that having a feminized chest did not make him any less of a man. He'd lived with that part of his body for four decades and was still a man, but he did not want to live with his chest for the next half of his life. He'd made the decision because it was his body … his choice. Then, in one act, Veronica had taken that choice away from him. Now, he wasn't facing another four decades in this same body. No, he was facing eternity. Anger and sadness battled inside him, and he didn't know which would win, but they both stayed with him in the end.

When the sun set, Jeffery unlocked the door and found Lucas sitting at the bottom of the closet, the binder still clutched between his fists and his face, unwilling to cry the tears he needed. Jeffery sunk next to him and put his arms around his shoulder. They sat in silence for a few minutes before Jeffery broke it.

"Why don't I go show you around the Ranch?"

"So I can get used to my prison?" The words came out harsher than Lucas intended, but he didn't take them back.

"I thought it would help take your mind off things."

"Because somehow that will make it better? I am stuck like this, and it is all her fault. And you want to tell me that it will all be better if I go walk around and look at the tennis courts or whatever other shit is waiting outside?" Lucas wanted to pull away and go on a rampage, getting out all his frustration, but Jeffery's arms were warm, and he found himself leaning into them.

"I'm not telling you that it will all be better. My experience was different. I chose this"

"Why? Why would you possibly want to be stuck like this?"

"I had a husband. It was 1960, so it wasn't legal. To everyone we knew, we were just two bachelors who lived together. I loved him and I know he loved me also. But he also had dreams, and those dreams required him to conform. One day, he moved out without a word. He didn't even leave a note. Three months later, he was getting married to his boss's daughter. He came back once. As we lay in each other's arms, he told me how much he missed me and wished there was another way. The next day, his first daughter was born. I petitioned to get changed the day after. No one should be ashamed of who they are or who they love, or for not loving anyone at all."

"I'm glad it worked out for you," Lucas said. He threw the binder back in the closet, stood up, and walked to the other side of the room, as far away from Jeffery as possible.

"I can't understand how it feels, but others here can." Jeffery stood up and walked out of the closet but stayed on the other side of the bedroom. "They know what it is like to be trapped without choice in a body they did not want, for eternity. Maybe talking to one of them will help."

"Were they able to change?"

"What?"

"Are they still stuck, or were they able to change?"

"They are still unchanged. It isn't always easy, but they have found ways to come to terms with it over time. Some have even turned it into an advantage."

Jeffery moved closer, but Lucas pulled away. "Please don't. Don't touch me. I just … I don't want to be here. I don't want to be *this*."

"Okay, I hear you. I can't change who you are or your situation, but how about a change of scenery?"

Lucas eyed him warily before deciding to follow him.

R ocko's was still the same. Lucas half expected the world to have changed as much as he had, but the women with the pixie cuts were in the corner, and the group of jocks were still playing pool and darts. Even Mika sat at the same table with her customary scowl in place.

When they entered, the bar turned to look at them as if they all knew what walked through the door. Or maybe it was instinct. There were humans here. Lucas could sense them, the smell of their skin and the beating of their hearts. However, they were few compared to the other creatures. The jocks in the corner with racing hearts that smelled like wet fur carried a scent that was so repulsive he knew that they were not food. And over at the table was Mika. She smelled slightly burnt with a heartbeat that only sped up because of the sight of him. He knew she could be fed on in an emergency, but it wouldn't be enjoyable.

Mika stared back at him, as if deciding whether she needed to take action. The stare was enough to remind Lucas of who he was and the thoughts running through his head. He put his hand up to his forehead and closed his eyes, trying to reset himself. The sounds and smells were still there, but they no longer overwhelmed him. When he opened his eyes, Mika gave him one last look and returned to shooting daggers at her beer.

Jeffery guided them to the bar. Even though it was standing room only, the way seemed to open for them magically, and two seats appeared for them to sit on. Lucas tried to look around to see who'd given the seats up, but everyone in the bar seemed to be paying as little attention to the duo as possible.

Without Lucas, Rocko was behind the bar serving customers. Guilt tugged on him for not showing up for his shift, even if it hadn't been his choice.

"I'm sorry," Lucas said. "I didn't have any way to call and tell you I needed to quit."

But Rocko ignored him and turned to address Jeffery instead. "Are you sure it is safe for him to be out this early?"

"He did fine last night. You let him stay the whole shift."

Lucas turned and looked at Rocko. Something was missing, and he couldn't figure out what.

"He hadn't finished then."

"He still hasn't. There is another week or two before his body will fully adjust. Even then, you know as well as most that we do not turn into monsters unless we want to."

"I'm not worrying about him hurting anyone. This is a mixed-species bar. I want to make sure he doesn't call attention."

All at once, it hit Lucas. Rocko had no heartbeat, and he smelled like dirt. If Lucas closed his eyes, he wouldn't have been able to tell there was a person standing there at all. What was he? Then, the conversation caught up to him, and a realization finally hit him.

"Wait, you know?" Lucas said.

"I didn't know she was targeting you. I would have found a way to stop it. Kin or not, being my employee and under the protection of my people should have been enough for her request to have been denied. I already have a complaint filed with the council. Not that it will do you much good."

Lucas's mind started to spin. Rocko knew who Veronica was and had let her play with him. Mika had warned him, but not enough to stop what had happened. This bar had never been his haven. It'd been a refuge for a world he should have never known about.

"I'm hoping being in a place that he has found comfort from, around his found family, will help. It has been a hard transition. Do you mind if we stay for a bit?" Jeffery threw some bills on the counter, and Rocko filled two wineglasses with water and brought them over.

Except this was not his family. Lucas glanced at Jeffery, trying to tell him they needed to leave without making him say the words. They would crush Rocko, and, despite everything, Lucas couldn't do that.

Jeffery reached out and held his hand tight, and Lucas felt the tension release.

Rocko put down a glass of water in front of Lucas. He gave an apologetic shrug that moved his entire body. "You can't drink it. I won't let perfectly good wine go to waste when all you need is a prop."

Lucas let out a sigh and then took his glass in his hands. Rocko moved off to help other customers, and Lucas's eyes followed him. Then he looked around the bar at the mix of characters. The pixie women's hearts beat so fast it reminded him of humming-birds. There were the Jamisons, an older couple who frequented the bar. Lucas had watched the men dote on each other, giving him hope that one day he would have something similar. Now he noticed they gave off a slight dampness he'd never noticed before. Maybe he hadn't known everything about this bar; he still didn't. But these people accepted him for who he was, both as a trans human and now a vampire. The least he could do was accept them back.

Lucas returned his attention to Jeffrey. "What would happen if we tried to drink it?"

"There is no more digestion. It would sit in your stomach."

"But Veronica came in here and drank."

Jeffery raised his eyebrows in an exaggerated question. "Are you sure?"

Lucas replayed the scenes in the bar, careful not to remember what came after. She'd put the cup to her lips a few times, and eventually, the contents of the cup disappeared, but he couldn't say with certainty that he'd actually seen her drinking any of it. "So, it would just sit there until my stomach exploded?"

"You are so dramatic." Jefferey's free hand came up and caressed his cheek. Lucas found himself leaning into the warmth. "No, the stomach is very elastic. It would stretch and rot until you began to stink from the inside. Your belly would start to bulge out, and eventually, one of the nurses would need to go in and drain you. I have been told it is not a pleasant experience. Vampires who have it done once usually do not even pretend to eat food afterward."

Lucas looked down at his cup and then pushed it away from him.

"Would you like to dance?" Jeffery asked.

Lucas looked up, surprised at being asked.

"Unless you would rather go ask that stunning witch over there. She hasn't kept her eyes off of you since we entered."

Lucas glanced over and saw Mika watching them with her signature scowl.

"Mika is gay," Lucas said. "So am I." Then the words caught up with him. "Wait, she is a witch? Is that how she knew what Veronica was?"

"That and she went to school with one of her granddaughters. I don't think they got along very well. But I didn't know she was gay. I bet the coven loves that. They are less accepting than even humans. They think everything has to be binary and that binaries attract. Like the world hasn't shown time and time again that that is not the case. Now, shall we dance?"

It'd been a while since Lucas had danced with someone, and never in public. Jeffery took his hand and guided him over to the jukebox. He typed in three songs and gave Lucas a wink as he led him to the floor. Not too many people were dancing. Most were standing around, but they managed to rearrange themselves enough that there was space for Jeffery and Lucas to move.

The first song was fast, and the two men danced around each other, neither with much talent. By the end, Lucas was laughing, the weight of the situation having lightened.

The second song was a sexy tempo, and Jeffery slid his body right next to Lucas. Lucas felt his body responding, and he grinned right along with Jeffery. The third song was slower, and they gathered each other in their arms. Lucas was ready to find a back room or return to the Ranch to resolve the tension. At least he knew that vampires were still capable of sex. Jeffery's testament to that pressed against him.

Their faces were next to each other, both about the same height, and Lucas wasn't sure who made the first move, just that their lips met, and then their tongues and hands began to roam. It was too much for a public dance floor, and if Lucas's brain hadn't shut down and his libido taken over, he might have recognized that. Instead, he pulled back slightly, leaving Jeffery's bottom lip in his mouth as he gently nipped on it. Then he moved to the side of his neck, kissing and nibbling all the way down. He didn't stop until he noticed one of the jocks staring at him.

The jock began tapping his friends' shoulders, calling for attention and pointing right at them or, rather, at Jeffery's neck. Lucas turned and noticed two rows of dots trailing down his skin. He put his hand to his mouth and found two extended canines.

Jeffery's eyes had been closed, lost in ecstasy, until Lucas stopped. When Jeffery opened his eyes, he looked at Lucas, and his eyes widened in surprise. He reached into his back pocket and put a pair of sunglasses on him despite it being night and them being inside. Then he kissed him, his lips helping cover up the fangs. With an intoxicating fluidity, Jeffery reached up his finger like he was allowing him to bite it and fixed Luca's lips so they temporarily covered up the fangs.

At that moment, Rocko appeared beside them, forging a trail between the people.

"You both need to go ... now."

Jeffery clenched Lucas's hand and pulled him out the door before Lucas could even process what had happened. As Jeffery led them to their car, the green convertible they'd borrowed from the garage, Lucas reached up to feel his teeth, but the fangs were no longer there.

"What's wrong?" Lucas asked. "I've seen more provocative dancing in Rocko's before. Why do we have to leave? I thought it was safe there for us."

Jeffery opened the passenger door for Lucas and gestured for him to get in, but Lucas held firm, refusing to sit until he understood what had happened. Rocko's was his home, a home he was only now able to appreciate fully, and Jeffery was pulling him away from it.

"It wasn't the dancing," Jeffery relented. "It was the fangs."

"People already knew what we were. What difference did it make?"

"You worked at Rocko's for months and had no idea what was happening around you."

"Maybe I should have," Lucas said. He moved toward Jeffery and the open door. "Maybe if I'd known, I wouldn't have been turned."

"Maybe," Jeffery said. He let go of the car door and walked

toward the driver's side. "Things may have been different for you, but even that isn't guaranteed. Either way, what happened in there was a violation of the treaty."

"What treaty?"

"Get in, and I'll explain." Jeffery slid into the driver's seat without waiting for Lucas's answer.

With a resigned sigh, Lucas sat down and pulled his door shut.

"Seatbelt," Jeffery said as he put his own on.

Lucas turned and looked at him incredulously. "I figured a car accident wouldn't kill us."

"It probably wouldn't, but we still feel pain while we heal. I find it is best not to chance fate."

Lucas reached over and pulled on his seatbelt as they drove out of the parking lot and headed back toward the Ranch.

"Ember is a hub of different species, none of which humans can know actually exist. We manage to live together without war because of the treaty signed centuries ago. You can almost say that we are a social experiment. Most hubs are held by one species; when a species tries to take it over, there is war. Here in Ember, we coexist. There have been a few other cities that have tried the same model, and we hope more will continue. With human technology, it is already getting harder to live undetected. It is imperative that we do nothing to put the treaty at risk."

"It wasn't that bad, was it? If anyone asks, we can pretend it was fake Halloween fangs."

"It isn't just you; the balance has been precarious for a while now. It just isn't the time to test it, especially not at a mixed establishment."

Lucas sunk back in his seat. He hadn't had an injection of his testosterone, but he could feel it in his system. A new permanent feature. It was a comfort amid the chaos, but it was another change. When he'd first gone on testosterone, the doctor joked about experiencing a second puberty, and he had. Lucas needed to relearn who he was and how to respond all over again. But it was worth it to finally see himself reflected back from the mirror.

Now, it felt like he was experiencing a third puberty, one he didn't want and which moved him further from who he wanted to be. There was more than just the mix of hormones; there was the pull he still felt from his human self and the new urges that were springing up as he came closer to finishing the transition.

Jeffery's hand reached over and grasped Lucas's, their fingers intertwining. All the turmoil inside of Lucas calmed at the gesture. They held on to each other as they drove back and parked.

"It will be okay," Jeffery said as he pulled between two parked cars. "I will be here to help as much as possible."

But Lucas wondered how much he would be allowed to. As soon as they exited the car, there was another vampire, one with pasty white skin, a lanky build, and dressed entirely in black. It seemed so cliche that Lucas had to make an effort not to laugh.

"You are wanted," the new vampire said.

Jeffery gave Lucas a brief glance that he couldn't interpret, then reached for his hand again.

"Not the infant. He is to go to his room and wait. You are to see the mistress."

Jeffery turned to Lucas. "Everything will be just fine," he said, but his tone suggested that he was just as nervous as Lucas was. "You will help him back to his room. He doesn't know the way."

Lucas watched as Jeffery walked through the door that connected to the house. The other vampire stood utterly still, not even bothering to blink.

"I'm Lucas."

The vampire looked at him in disgust. When Jeffery was completely gone, the vampire moved away so fast that Lucas only knew he moved because the door opened and was left to slam shut on its own.

"No need to worry about me," he muttered to the empty garage, and began to make his own way to the house.

In the nighttime, the house had become more lively. There were sounds behind rooms and a few people drifting through the halls. He tried to stop someone who appeared to be in their mid-twenties wearing the outfit of a twenties flapper girl to ask for directions, but she flashed her fangs at him and shuffled off.

On instinct, Lucas touched his mouth and was happy to see that his fangs stayed hidden. He put his finger in his mouth, trying to determine where they'd come from, but his canines were the same as when he'd been a human. There was no hidden second set that he could feel.

With a sigh, he continued walking. When he passed by what looked like a community room with vampires sitting around reading or watching television, he stopped at the doorway, trying to determine the best way to approach them. But he didn't have to worry. They all turned toward him, staring without initiating conversation.

"Hi," Lucas said. "I'm new. I'm trying to find my way to my room. I think it is on the third floor. Any chance you can point me in the direction of the stairs?"

"Is that the one causing us all the trouble?" The vampire who spoke was sitting on one of the couches, a book in his lap. He was dressed in a suit and tie, looking like he was late for some big corporate meeting.

"Must be," said a second vampire, who seemed young—not more than eighteen. She was lying on her stomach on the couch, flipping through stations on the 72-inch television. She turned her head back to the TV, Lucas forgotten, and started kicking her feet up and down as she watched a reality show.

Lucas turned to the third person in the room. The woman was sitting at a chessboard but had already shifted her attention back to the pieces before her. The businessman scowled and returned to his book.

"Awesome," Lucas muttered before continuing his search. Eventually, he found his way to the stairs hidden behind a set of doors. On the third floor, he wandered, trying to remember the way to his quarters, but he became distracted by an empty library. He looked at the hundreds of volumes from across the generations before finally settling on a relatively new release. It was a mystery and was supposed to be very good. Now that he had the time, he might as well catch up on his reading.

Unsure what else to do, he began trying doors as he walked down the halls. Some were locked. Others were empty. A few held vampires who hissed at him when he opened the door. He quickly closed those and continued on his way. Eventually, he saw a room that was familiar and walked in. He settled on the couch and started to read. There was nothing else to do anyway.

I t was hours before Jeffery returned. Lucas had finished the book and paced around the room, finally locating a TV hidden behind a set of wooden doors. He turned it on and wasn't surprised to find morning talk shows. He laid on the couch and watched a cooking segment about new ways to cook eggs.

When his door opened, Lucas didn't even bother moving. He figured it didn't matter who it was at this point, but he wasn't surprised when Jeffery sat on the couch by his feet. The two watched the traffic report for the Denver area, even though the larger city was too far away for anything there to impact them.

"What happened?" Lucas finally asked. He shut off the TV and sat up facing Jeffery.

"I should have been more careful. You are still young, and I should have realized that you would not have the ability to control your instincts."

"Control them? I don't even know what happened. Somehow, there were fangs. But now, nothing." Lucas opened up his mouth, showing Jeffrey human-looking teeth.

Jeffery let out a light chuckle. "I'm sorry, you just look so cute when you're frustrated. The teeth expand coming in when you need them. Scientists think it is an evolutionary adaptation that allows us to get the blood we need while helping us remain hidden within society. You will learn control. I shouldn't have taken you out so early."

"I'm glad you did," Lucas said. "I know what happened wasn't good, but being happy for a few minutes was nice."

Jeffery reached for Lucas, pulling him until Lucas was straddling his lap. The two kissed, and all the feelings in the club came rushing back. Lucas was not surprised to reach up and find that his fangs were again extended. He touched the top button on Jeffery's shirt and waited until Jeffery nodded in assent before he unbuttoned it and then each one after. He did it slowly, his hands trailing down Jeffery's bare chest as he moved to the next button. When he was done, he leaned back and looked at what he saw. Jeffery was slender, and while there was no six-pack, there was some tone that Lucas found irresistible.

"You are so sexy," Lucas muttered before leaning down to kiss Jeffery once again.

As they kissed, Jeffery's hands crept up under Lucas's shirt, pulling the shirt up higher until his hands rubbed over his binder, the shirt bundling near his neck, ready to come off. Lucas pulled back and grabbed his shirt, putting it securely back on.

"You don't need to take it off," Jeffery said. "I won't do anything you aren't comfortable with. I happen to think you are a very sexy man."

Lucas grabbed the hem of his shirt, playing with it before leaving it in place. He leaned in, letting his clothed chest rest against Jeffery's. They kissed like their lives depended on it, not stopping even as Jeffery stood up and carried Lucas into the bedroom.

"So that's why there is a bed," Lucas mumbled, his lips still intertwined with Jeffery's.

It was later, when they were both mostly naked and content, that Jeffery told Lucas what had happened.

"So the jocks are werewolves? Like actual humans that can shift to wolves?"

"Yep."

"How many other creatures are out there, and how have I never noticed them before?"

"There are more than you can imagine. Most live on their own, far away from humans, if possible. In Ember, there are more than two dozen different species. It is the most diverse city in the magical community."

"Because it is a gathering ground?" Lucas's fingers caressed Jeffery's lower back as he lay in the crook of his arm.

"It is a nexus, yes. I believe you may know them as ley lines, places where webs of magic come together to create a pool of magical energy." Jeffery's hand rested where Lucas's shirt had been pulled up.

"So these wolves are upset?" Lucas asked.

"Do you remember the treaty I mentioned? Since vampires have long lifespans, the wolves are concerned about us outnumbering them. It is unfounded. We are limited. Kin must choose to be turned. But the treaty helps them to feel better and gives our kind a safety most other hordes do not have. The treaty requires all kin who wish to be turned to apply to the council."

"I didn't do that, and now it is causing problems?"

Jeffery shrugged, his head bobbing slightly against Lucas's chest.

"There is going to be a town hall meeting to discuss the circumstances of your turning. We need to prove that what happened was an accident and not a violation of the treaty."

"So this meeting is a formality? A way for them to complain. I don't need to worry?"

"You don't need to worry." Jeffery trailed his fingers down Lucas's chest as he spoke. "Your transformation was outside of your control. However, the wolves may twist this to get something out of the council. We aren't sure what their aim is. They are control freaks, though. They may just be upset that they weren't allowed to give their approval."

They lounged together in the bed for hours. Jeffery seemed to have an uncanny sense of time; without any indication that something had changed, he leaned up and kissed Lucas. "We need to get ready."

The shower came in handy. There was no sweat or bodily fluids, but it did help to wash off the lube and oils they'd used. It was also perfectly sized for the two of them to enjoy.

Once they were out, Jeffery threw on his old clothes and left to prepare. Lucas stared at his closet, wondering what one wore to a council meeting when the topic up for discussion was your very existence.

He finally decided on some nice black jeans and a button-down shirt. It must have been good enough. When Jeffery came to collect him, Lucas got a nod of approval before they headed down to one of the cars.

The council building was on the other side of town, past all the residential houses, with long stretches of grass between buildings. The building was unassuming, just a barn-like structure with a large parking lot already filled by the time Jeffery pulled in. They parked near the back, and as they walked in, Lucas noticed that there wasn't a junker anywhere in the parking lot.

"Are all paranormal creatures rich?"

"No, some choose to own nothing, but the ones you see here all have long family traditions. They have wealth handed down and long lives to earn more. They wouldn't let anyone here know, even if they did have financial troubles. They would bring out their finest to make everyone think all was well. There is a lot of show in the truce that the nations have."

The building ended up being one room with a high ceiling. Ten beings, each from a different species, were seated on a raised platform. Lucas looked for the vampire representative and found a child who appeared to be no more than eight years old. Lucas turned and looked at Jeffery in surprise.

"There weren't always the same rules," he said. "She is older than us all and leads the vampire council."

Lucas nodded, uncertain how to respond. The thought of

being trapped in the body of a child was more than he could comprehend, and to know that that child was the oldest of them … didn't change Lucas's situation. Still, he better understood why Jeffery had mentioned that others would sympathize with the discomfort he felt.

"It has come to our attention that a kin has been changed without going through the proper steps to receive authorization from the council." The man had to have been at least six-foot-five, and even if he hadn't stood up to speak, he would have towered over most of the council members. He was older, the signs starting to show in the graying of his hair, but his body still looked agile.

"That is the alpha," Jeffery whispered. "That is his pack."

Lucas turned and looked at a group standing in the front right of the room. It was full of the men that Lucas had seen in the bar, including the one that Lucas remembered from the coffee shop the morning that he found out what he'd become. It left him wondering how it had taken until his fangs had come out at the bar for the alpha to know about his existence. Mixed in with the group was one female who was shorter than the rest but just as athletic. She wore a pair of headphones over her ears but still seemed to wince every time a loud noise was made.

"I demand to know how this happened!" the alpha screamed. Lucas noticed the werewolf woman flinch and cup her hands over the headphones, as if trying to fuse them to her face.

"I assure you that this change was accidental." The vampire leader's voice was squeaky and high-pitched. "A bloodletting permit was applied for and approved. He was a visitor from out of town, and there was no connection to him being kin. It was an unfortunate accident that will not happen again." She did not bother trying to stand up or intimidate the alpha with size. She remained sitting in a chair that looked to have been made specifically for her, the bottom raised to put her high enough to be above the table, even though she was still shorter than everyone else. If it bothered her, it did not come across. She spoke as if she had authority and expected everyone else to respect it, as if it was a given that she ruled. "Veronica will explain."

Veronica walked to the stage, facing the council members. She addressed them as if there was no one else in the room.

"I first located the turned while he was working in Rocko's bar. That same night, I applied for a bloodletting permit." She spoke dispassionately, as if this was just an annoyance. "As the turned had only recently arrived in our city, I went back to ask some follow-up questions about his origins. He mentioned that he'd been born and raised in California, and no connection with kin was found. My permit was granted.

"That same night, nearing morning, I approached the turned easily. Everything went as expected. He had no memories of the event, and I returned him to his apartment where he would be safe until he woke the next morning without any knowledge of what had happened."

That night flooded back to Lucas. The confusion and pain as the teeth tore into his neck. The scream that was cut off by her hand holding him still. The loss of control and inability to stop her from taking what he did not want to give. Lucas put his hands to his eyes, willing the images to disappear. He must have let out a cry because he found Jeffery's arms around him, holding him, and heard the alpha speak up.

"It appears that he remembered after all."

"Yes, it does," Veronica said quietly. "I was unaware."

Lucas tried to pull himself together. He could feel the eyes of everyone in the room on him, and somehow, he knew that it was vital for him to present as stable. He thought he may not leave this room alive if he did not show that he was worthy. So he released his hands, took a deep breath, and turned his attention back to the council proceedings.

"If the vampire council was so thorough, how did it miss that he was kin?" the alpha said. "If they are incapable of protecting their own, then maybe that responsibility should be moved to the broader council."

Mutterings came from other council members and different groups in the room. This seemed to Lucas like a very unpopular idea.

"Don't worry," Jeffery whispered. "No one wants that idea to pass, except maybe the wolves. They are all worried about losing control of their communities. There is too much difference between them to find common ground in every aspect. It would descend into chaos."

"Then why would he even suggest it?" Lucas asked.

"Wolves are ruled by hierarchy. They need rules upon rules, and in their mind, everyone else is chaotic. They want to order and structure to the rest of Ember. I don't think the alpha realizes the disorder that would cause in the long run. It is bad enough that he refuses to step down. People won't put up with much more."

"Council," Veronica continued, "this was an unfortunate incident and one that will not happen again. We were looking for the wrong person. Lucas Johnson was not found to be kin, but B———— Altman was."

Lucas's hands bunched into fists; he let out a scream and went to rush Veronica. It was bad enough to turn him, but to mention that person, the person who was now as dead as her parents, was too much. Jeffery took hold of him and, even in Lucas's rage, held him back. The rest of the room continued as if he hadn't even reacted.

"B———— Altman was the daughter of Elizabeth Altman and Henry Altman. After they had their daughter, both signed away their right to be turned and applied for and were granted permission to relocate. They moved to California to be near friends that the pair had met in college. Shortly after their move, the pair died in a car crash. This was recorded. It was also recorded that their daughter was adopted. She now became known as B———— Jackson. B———— Jackson went on to marry Gregory Samuel, and she changed her name to B———— Samuel. They divorced last year, and all traces of B———— Samuel disappeared. She was on a watch list for the trackers to find so the records could be updated. No one had any idea that B——— Samuel had become Lucas Johnson. There was no reason to connect the two people."

Never before had Lucas wished to be able to lose control. He needed some way to deal with all these emotions. His whole life had been summed up and broadcast to a room of people he didn't know. Veronica spoke like she was reading a boring book report, but she was talking about his birth parents and the accident that he still vaguely remembered. Also, his adoptive mom, their close friend, who'd taken him in. Even before he'd come out to her, she had hugged him and called him her son. Then, there was his marriage, the last failure in a life of misfortune. After he'd packed up his bags and headed to the small town of Ember, CO, in some vague attempt to connect to his birth parents. His birth parents who were apparently vampire kin.

"Fuck," he said just loud enough for Jeffery to hear. "I didn't know. There was no way for me to know. She was just some creep at a bar asking too many personal questions."

"No one blames you," Jeffery said.

But Lucas looked out at the room. They all seemed very much to blame him.

"I don't understand," the alpha said, now less worried about control and more confused about what he had just heard. "What does this girl have to do with the man who was turned?"

"I can't," Lucas said. He moved off to the door and went out into the night. Lucas walked around the building to the side opposite the parking lot and crossed the street to a field of tall grass. He ran into it, bundling down as far as he could go, trying to escape from the conversation happening in the building. Here was yet another place that wouldn't accept him for who he was. At least a hundred people had heard, and most everyone else would know by the end of the night. Somehow, it would make it over to the humans, and soon, he wouldn't be able to walk through town without everyone knowing. Not that the vampires would allow him to walk through town anytime soon, anyway.

He had no control over his life anymore. He belonged to a group that had thrown out his personal information at their whim with no concern for the impact on him. A group of people that gave another permission to take his blood, to freeze him at this point in his life forever. Whether they meant for it to happen didn't matter. They permitted it all the same.

And now it all pressed on him: the car crash and seeing his parents' lifeless bodies as he waited hours for help, the name that had haunted him until he'd finally thought he was free of it, and the night where his future had been taken from him. They spiraled together, and he couldn't even pass out from the pain of it; no tears could come; he just sat frozen, immobile, unable to escape.

Jeffery found Lucas in the grass, unmoving. After all, why did he need to move? He was a vampire now. He didn't need to eat or breathe. Why should he bother moving?

Lucas didn't want to know what had happened in the meeting after he'd left because that would mean discussing everything else. All his pain had been laid bare for others, even Jeffery.

Jeffery lay down next to Lucas, and the two men silently watched the sky.

"Did you know?" Lucas finally said.

"I knew after we came back from the bar. They told me what they found out."

"And you let them … tell everyone?"

"No. It wasn't supposed to happen like that. That was heartless. After you left the meeting, she was called out for her behavior in front of everyone. Not just by me but by our council lead and even the alpha wolf, once he understood what she was trying to say."

"But it doesn't matter because she accomplished exactly what she wanted. Now everyone knows everything," Lucas said.

"Yes."

Lucas appreciated that Jeffery didn't try to sugarcoat it. It sucked, just like being stuck in this body sucked, but it was all too much.

"So, did they make a decision?"

"They did," Jeffery said. "They determined that due to the extenuating factors and since there has not been a qualifying candidate for turning in some time, the werewolves will take back their claim, on the condition that Veronica is responsible for your upbringing and actions from here on out."

"They made her my sponsor?"

"Yes. I tried to volunteer, but I was deemed too young."

"It doesn't matter," Lucas said, shoving all the hurt and pain as far down inside him as it could go. "It's done. I can't change any of this, so I better accept it and move on."

He tried to will himself to believe it, and some part of him could if he didn't think too hard.

"I guess that means there is only one thing left to do," Lucas said.

"What is that?" Jeffery asked.

"Figure out who killed my parents."

"Wait, what?" Jeffery stood up and started pacing, knocking down the tall grass to make room. "Why do you think your parents were murdered?"

"You heard Veronica. My parents decided to leave the control of this city, and not even a year later, they ended up killed in a car accident. There was no bad weather, no known cause for why they hit the median, and smashed in the front of the car. They were killed instantly. It'd always felt like it couldn't have been an accident, and now I finally know why."

"The vampires didn't order a hit on your parents. They wouldn't have allowed them to leave if they hadn't been okay with them leaving. I'm sorry, but it was an accident."

"Would they tell you if they had?"

Jeffery stared at him with sympathy in his eyes. "Let's go back to the Ranch. I can finally give you a tour and introduce you to the other vampires." He held out his hand, and Lucas took it. They walked back to the council building, but as they strode by, the vampire council representative called out for Jeffery.

"Do you mind if I take the keys?" Lucas asked. "I don't want to stand around outside."

Veronica was currently talking to the vampire council lead. The childlike figure chewing out the tall woman could have been comical in another situation.

For now, Lucas took the keys and walked toward the car, a silver sedan, one of the simpler cars that didn't outshine any of the council members. His brain was on autopilot, too over-whelmed with the last few days to think or feel. Nothing made sense anymore, and Lucas needed it to make sense. He needed his change to have a reason, and maybe that reason was to help out the parents he barely knew.

Lucas unlocked the door and slid into the driver's seat. He hadn't driven since arriving in this town. When he had realized he would not need his car to get around, he had sold it for five hundred dollars, which had gone to pay for the doctor's visit and a new testosterone prescription. It had been worth it. Lucas could not imagine the situation he would be in if he had been turned even a year earlier, his face still full of feminine curves.

He put the key into the ignition, started the car, and was out of the parking lot leaving everyone behind.

Lucas parked a block over from the bar in a parking lot belonging to a hardware store that had closed for the night. He hoped that it would prevent the vampires from seeing the car right away and realizing where he'd gone.

Then he walked the last block to Rocko's. It was quiet inside, and Lucas realized at least some of the clientele would have been at the council meeting. Behind the bar was a young man, not much more than twenty-one. Lucas had been replaced. He'd known it would need to happen, but it didn't help the sting of seeing it. He buried it down with the rest of the pain.

The man's heartbeat was sluggish, and he smelled faintly of rot. He was undoubtedly a supernatural creature, but not one Lucas had met before.

"What can I get you?" the man asked.

That was supposed to be Lucas's line. It'd been stolen from him along with everything else.

"Is Rocko here?"

The man went into the kitchen and returned a minute later with Rocko. Rocko's look of surprise was almost enough to tear Lucas apart.

"What are you doing here?"

"I need some information."

Rocko ushered Lucas up the stairs to his living quarters. The place was as unused as ever, and Lucas sat carefully on the small bed while Rocko plopped down onto an overlarge chair, the only piece of furniture that could hold his bulk.

"I heard what happened," Rocko said.

"That was fast."

"I own a bar. Gossip is part of the job."

"That is just great." Lucas slumped down, burying his head in his hands.

"I assume they did not let you come here?"

"They also didn't specifically tell me I couldn't come here."

Rocko hesitated at Lucas's confession. The mood tensed as the older man decided how to proceed. "So what do you want?"

Lucas relaxed once he realized that Rocko would not throw him out. "You know about them, about all of them. Your bar is supernatural as much as a queer bar."

"I like to think of it as both, but everyone is welcome as long as they are respectful. I wouldn't use 'supernatural'; it isn't well received."

"Then what should I say?"

"It isn't one community. We are all a bunch of smaller communities. The only thing we have in common is magic of one form or another. Well, two things: we hide from humans. If you must group everyone, then 'the magical community' will do."

"We? So you are part as well?" Lucas stood up and started pacing the small room, surprised at Rocko's admission.

"I am a rock troll. The last of my family. I got lonely, so I opened the bar."

"A troll."

"Yes, we have a bad rap in human myths, but we are quite friendly most of the time."

"And there are other creatures that all live here in Ember because it is magical?" Lucas asked.

"That is the short version, but ultimately true. The vampires should have taught you all this by now."

Lucas ignored Rocko's question and went forward with his train of thought. "And what would happen if someone wanted to leave?"

"Why do I think you are talking about something specific?" Rocko asked.

"You heard everything that happened tonight?"

"Yes."

"So, you heard about my parents. They are kin who decided to leave. Then, a year later, they were in an unexplained accident."

"You think something happened?" Rocko's voice was full of disbelief.

"Doesn't it seem likely? Maybe some vampires weren't happy that they left and decided to teach them a lesson. Maybe they had problems with them raising a child far away from vampires."

Rocko got up and put a hand on Lucas's shoulder, which caused him to stand still.

"Your parents would have told you about the vampires when you were older. The families who leave come back when their kids are teenagers and old enough to know to keep their mouths shut. And yes, it happens all the time. Your parents were not special; they were the norm. Families decide they don't want to raise their kids here and strike out somewhere else. Then, kids come back to raise their kids at the slower pace of a small town. It is a cycle that I have seen happen time and time again. It is why the vampires keep such intricate records. I don't think they would have done anything to your parents. It was an accident, an unfortunate accident."

"It can't be. It has to be their fault. Don't you see? This is why I was turned. As a vampire, I can finally solve my parents' murder. "

Rocko placed his other hand on Lucas's other shoulder, causing the vampire to face him as he spoke. "You think Veronica turned you because she wants you to solve a murder?"

"No, not Veronica. Fate caused this, maybe with the help of my parents' ghosts. There have to be ghosts, right?"

"A lot has happened to you recently, my friend. I should call the Ranch."

"Don't. Please don't." Lucas started to tremble. "I need to do this. If you have seen parents bringing their children back repeatedly, does that mean you were here? Did you know my parents?"

Rocko grew sad at these words. "I wasn't in this community then. I was in another. I lived with my mother and my father. Those of us who cannot have children stay and help raise the young, but my parents had no other children, and no family members needed help with their young. So I moved here instead. It was too hard to see my parents everywhere and to be left with no other close family. When I saw that others were not as accepting as my kind of those who love others like themselves or, like me, who do not desire that kind of love and connection at all, I decided to open up Rocko's. I have only been here in this community for fifteen years, not long enough to have known your parents.

"I'm sorry that you also lost your parents." Lucas sunk back onto the bed.

"It is hard, but my parents had a long life and returned to the mountain when it was their time. I miss them, but it was not sad, not like parents who were taken before their time. I understand why you are angry, but I do not think they were taken from you. It was an accident, an unfortunate accident."

"But someone had to have been around then who would know. Someone I could talk to that is not connected to the council."

"The only people I can think of are the nymphs in the forest, but they will not talk to you."

"Why not?"

"They are an intolerant people that only see femininity. If they have a son, they send him away, never to be spoken about. They would not be happy to talk to a man. Especially one born into what they view as a superior form."

Lucas froze in indecision and at seeking out a group of people who would hate him for who he was. He'd seen too much hate already and wasn't sure he could handle any more that day. Finally, he stood up, his decision made. "If they could know the answer, I must at least try."

The nymphs lived on the same side of the river as the bar, only further on the outskirts of town. In the quiet of the night, it only took Lucas ten minutes to drive there, but it took another fifteen minutes of turning around until he found the place to park that Rocko'd given him directions to.

The area was covered in tall trees with branches full of green needles that looked like they lived for hundreds of years. He walked, staying on the dirt path and keeping his hands in his pockets so as not to touch the trees, as Rocko had instructed. The Nymphs, apparently, became very upset if you did that. Not that he could blame them if the tree were their souls.

He expected the women to be nearby, maybe watching him while they perched on their trees or, half-wood themselves, living inside the trunks. Instead, it was just a forest. Not that he'd visited many forests. He wasn't great with the outdoors. There hadn't been a lot of woods in Los Angeles when he'd grown up, but he'd enjoyed the peace he'd felt walking beneath their branches.

Part of him wondered if there was magic trying to lure him to sleep, or at least into complicity. He discovered anything was possible, and it seemed premature to rule anything out. Lucas stayed vigilant until he saw the turnoff hidden between the trees, which he'd only noticed because Rocko had told him to look out for the blue wildflowers growing at the base of the trunk. The flowers were striking and entirely out of place.

He turned on the new path and began to hear music. The path opened to a clearing where nearly a hundred women were gathered on the lake's edge. Blankets of food surrounded them. Some danced, others sang, and a few played various instruments. Lucas picked out a flute and what looked like a lute. Some of the women were naked; others were dressed in different clothing: dresses of various lengths, bikinis, and anything that could be considered feminine.

The women looked to be in their early teens to late forties. Most had long flowing hair that looked like silk, although there were a few with shorter hair that was cut in such a way to accentuate femininity. Lucas spent most of his life trying to hide what they were revealing: the beauty of the female form. It was not until after his transition that he'd realized that he had nothing against the female form. He just did not want it to apply to him.

He stepped into the clearing, uncertain who was the best person to approach, but the entire group paused at his entrance. The night grew extra silent with the lack of music. Even the forest sounds seemed to have disappeared. A woman stood up; she was one of the older women, maybe in middle age, but Lucas now knew that in the magic world, that did not mean what it did in the human world. She wore a white dress that cut down her chest, split up her sides, and was cinched around the waist with a simple golden belt. It looked a bit cliche to Lucas, but then he was gay and didn't understand the appeal of women.

She sauntered up to him, making sure to move her hips as if she was performing some mating ritual, one in which the woman devoured the man at the end.

"Look what wandered in," she purred.

Lucas couldn't help himself. He rolled his eyes, let out a deep breath, and stood as patiently as he could while he waited for her to finish the routine.

The woman stopped and raised an eyebrow. Then she

continued toward him, no longer trying to seduce, but more like the predator that she was.

When she reached him, she asked, "What are you?" The woman grabbed his face, staring at him as if that would answer all her questions. It must have because one second, she was next to him, and the next, she was six feet away, every ounce of herself alert, showing how dangerous she could be. All the women were beside her, a hundred facing him, ready to pounce.

"Vampire," she hissed.

"Yes, but not by choice. This was done to me without my approval. I was hoping that you could help me. I need someone with a long memory not connected to the vampires."

"Out!" she screamed. There was nothing sexual about her any longer. It was as if she'd turned into anger, her eyes too large and her mouth opening wide when she spoke. She stood, taking up space, her arms stretched and her legs assuming a big, solid stance.

"Please, I need your help. There is no one else that I can turn to."

"Why should we help you?" she asked.

"Being this way was not my choice. I don't trust vampires or how they have little disregard for anyone other than themselves. I need help figuring out what happened to my parents. I need to know why they died."

"You are the new creation? The one that was born a female and gave it up to be … that?" She gestured at him vaguely.

"I didn't give up anything. This is who I was always meant to be. It doesn't matter what my body looks like; I have always been a man."

"You were given the greatest gift and turned your back on it. Women are power, and you walked away." She started to change again right before him. The monstrous creature went back into the picture of femininity. "Why would I help someone like that?"

"I was never a woman," Lucas said.

"Do you know what we do with any sons that we have? We

put them in the river so we never see their cursed faces again. You come in here flaunting that you have turned your back on the gift you have been given and want something from us?"

She turned and walked away.

Lucas stood there, fuming angrily from everything she'd said. "You don't get to decide who I am."

"And you are no use to us," she said without turning around. "You are not something we can play with, nor are you one of us. Be gone."

Lucas felt pressure pushing on him as if expelling him from the area. Suddenly, he found himself on the path next to the blue flowers, only now the side path was no longer visible. He'd lost his chance.

His mind drifted to Jeffery and the easy way he accepted him for exactly who he was, no questions asked. He wondered how much trouble he would get in for Lucas stealing the car and running away. Except he wasn't ready to go back yet; he wasn't prepared to face the future laid out before him. So he continued down the main, non-magical path until it connected to the river. He found a large rock to sit on and watched the water. It was pretty, reflecting the light of the moon.

Lucas wasn't sure how long he sat there before noticing someone watching him. She seemed young, maybe in her early twenties. Her hair was cut short, one side shaved completely off, and the other hung straight down, covering her right eye. Her hair was black, her one visible eye was brown, and her skin was a light copper. She was dressed in jeans and a T-shirt as if this was a regular walk down to the riverside and she was a normal human. Lucas noticed her grace; she moved like the nymphs he'd just seen, even if she didn't look like one.

He eyed her, uncertain what she wanted and whether she was a friend, but he didn't move either. If she wanted him off the river, then she would at least have to ask him.

"Hi," she said.

It was so simple, and it caught Lucas entirely off guard. It sounded shy and uncertain.

"Hi," he said back.

"I'm sorry about my mother. She isn't sorry, but I am."

"Your mother?" Lucas studied her again. She had this look in her eye like she had something to say but was uncertain how to say it. He'd seen that look before. He'd carried it once himself. It was the expression you wore when you were questioning every-thing about yourself, but you didn't know the right place to start.

"Yeah," she said. "You don't get to pick your family."

He looked at her, uncertain if he should start the actual conver-sation or accept the apology and move on. Then he thought back to all the hurtful things that her mother had said, and he looked at this young woman and knew he had to try and help.

"I bet having a mother like that could be difficult."

"She does a lot for the family. She has led and protected them for over a century."

"A century, wow. A lot can change in a century."

The woman stood there as if trying to decide if she should continue or go back.

"Do you mind if I ask how old you are?" Lucas asked.

"I'm thirty-four," she said. "We age, just slowly. Not like vampires." She broke off as if uncertain about bringing it up.

"It's okay to ask whatever you want to ask. If I don't want to answer, I won't."

"How did you know?" the words rushed out of her.

"That I am a man?"

She nodded slightly and then looked around her to ensure they were alone.

"I always knew. I didn't always understand. When I was young, I was constantly told that I was not allowed to act like a boy, so I tried not to be, but it ate at me my whole life until I just couldn't be who they expected me to be anymore. I had wasted half my life, and the thought of continuing on the rest of my life that way was unbearable."

There was silence then, but the active kind where he could see her processing his words, testing them for correctness inside herself.

"Are you a man?" he asked.

"I …" she said. "I don't know."

"Are you a woman?" he asked.

"No," she said instantly, a shock coming over her face as the words left her mouth. Her hands covered her lips as if they could stop them from escaping after the fact.

"I won't tell anyone," Lucas said. "I promise. That is not something anyone else should tell except yourself when you are ready. Did you know there is more than just man and woman? Biological sex is so diverse and not as simple as people want you to believe. Gender is even more so. If you are not a man and not a woman, then maybe you are agender."

"Agender?"

"Some people do not have a gender identity at all, and that is agender. But it's not the only option; there are so many. Whatever fits for you is what gender you are, even if you don't think that it's possible. I don't know why nymphs are supposed to be female, but I know that humans are so very diverse, and so many people get as angry as your mom when people do not fit into the boxes they have created."

"Agender." The word wasn't spoken, as much as tasted and claimed.

"Is it true that every nymph has a tree, and that tree is their soul?"

"Yes, mine is in the newer part of the forest. I feel it everywhere I go, even when I go into the city. We are joined."

Lucas nodded, glad that he understood that part correctly. "Remember this: no matter what your mom says, not all nymphs are women. Because it seems you are just as much nymph as she is."

The nymph's mouth seemed to open, and they walked back to the camp, their mind no doubt whirling with the conversation.

Lucas remembered that feeling when he'd first realized as an adult that it was okay to be who he was. His husband had been trying on suits for a friend's wedding. Lucas was supposed to be trying on a dress, but he couldn't bring himself to do it. He kept running his hands over the suits and ties. One of the men helping his husband walked toward him, and Lucas quickly took his hand off the material and tried to pretend all was normal. The man looked at him and told him that if he wanted to wear a suit, he could. He used male pronouns, and Lucas couldn't help the smile that grew on his face.

The man took his measurements and got him a suit. They walked away with two suits that day, and when his husband didn't say a thing, he took it as a good sign, like maybe he understood.

Lucas watched the nymph walk away until they disappeared back into the trees. He realized he hadn't even stopped to ask their name, but the city was small, and they were sure to run into them again. After all, he now had eternity.

There were still a few hours of darkness left, and Lucas wasn't ready to head back to the car, so he decided to get off the rock and walk to the river's edge. The river was large when it ran through town, but it seemed to be even wider out here. The other side was not visible even with his improving eyesight.

The night was peaceful, though, and he was happy for the time to think. As he walked, he saw fish fins pop above the water. He stopped and watched, uncertain of what he was seeing. The more he looked, the more activity there seemed to be, but Lucas didn't understand what was happening. Finally, he decided it wasn't important and continued on his way.

Lucas walked a mile further down the coast of the river before he decided to turn around. He spent the time lost in thought, imagining his new life as a vampire. The conversation with the nymph leader reminded him that it didn't matter what his body looked like. He was as much a man now as he'd been ten years ago. Although, he was glad for the deeper voice and the masculinized tone that he was allowed to keep for eternity. He'd spent so much time focused on chest surgery that the idea of it not happening had physically hurt. If it were an option, he would have undergone the surgery right that second, but it wasn't. At least he didn't have to breathe, and his body would continually heal itself, meaning he could keep a binder on all the time. It wasn't ideal, but it was at least a solution.

From the corner of his eye, Lucas began noticing even more movement in the water. At first, he thought that maybe he'd encountered rapids or rocks causing all the commotion, but something was moving through the water at him very fast. That one thing became a group of things, and before he knew it, a human-like head broke from the water. It was followed by a human torso, the chest unrestricted from clothes. Looking closer, Lucas noticed slits on the side of the neck that looked like gills.

"Merpeople," he said in wonder, but at this point, he wouldn't be surprised if a Sasquatch walked from the forest right in front of him.

Soon, more heads emerged from the water until Lucas saw eleven people assembled in a formation resembling an arrow pointing straight at him.

The lead person opened their mouth and started talking very fast. It was a series of clicks formed by rapidly moving their tongue against the roof of their mouth. Occasionally, there was a vibration in their throat. Lucas was reasonably sure it was language, but didn't understand it. So, he stood there, frozen, uncertain of what to do.

"I don't understand," he finally said. He held his hands open so they could see he had nothing in them. Although, he didn't know if this would convey the same meaning to a species that seemed to live in water.

Suddenly, the figure reached out of the water, grabbed his ankle, and dragged him into the river. They kept holding on as they began to swim. Lucas breathed in once, his human habits still strong, and got a mouthful of water stuck in his lungs. It sat there stinging as he was dragged. His ankle was firmly in the hand of the merperson, and his head was behind, next to their tail. It was a long tail full of scales like one would find on a fish. It wasn't exceptionally pretty, but now and then, a bit of light would hit it, and it would shine. The tail was powerful, propelling the merperson forward. Lucas tried to maneuver his body away from being hit by its movement, but the water made it difficult.

He knew he should be strong enough to break away, but his muscles were not made for water, and he wasn't used to relying on his strength. Lucas could vaguely make out the forms of the people behind them, his eyes too focused on not being hit by the giant tale. It went on forever, and Lucas was certain that he was being brought to his death, except he wasn't sure how vampires could die.

He never found out where he was being taken. There was a commotion; he felt a yank on his leg and was set free, drifting on the river current. He tried to break the water's surface, but his swimming lessons had been confined to California swimming pools and not raging rivers. He could not get enough purchase to stop his momentum until his hands caught on a large rock. Lucas waited a moment, not having to worry about drowning, before pushing himself above the current. It was enough to see the bank of the river. He let go, swimming angled toward land, but still drifted down the river for some distance before he was able to climb on the bank. The water still filled Lucas's lungs, and he couldn't figure out how to expel it, so he tried to ignore the discomfort and take stock of where he was and what was happening.

There was a commotion a quarter mile up the river, and Lucas started running toward it. Soon, he heard a series of clicks and noises going back and forth. On the side of the river was Jeffery, completely wet, arguing with the merperson who had captured Lucas. Jeffery gestured toward Lucas, his gaze intensifying until the merperson threw their arms up in disgust. The group moved toward the middle of the river, their heads still visible. When they were a decent ways away, the merperson gave a loud hiss that couldn't be anything other than anger or threat, and they all dove back under the surface.

"I'm sorry," Lucas said.

Jeffery stared back at him, motionless, and Lucas realized he'd pushed the man too far. Jeffrey looked him up and down as if to make sure he was whole and then started walking away, dripping water as he went. Lucas stayed, uncertain if he should follow, but he turned to the river, saw faces still watching him, and hurried after Jeffery.

They walked in silence until they reached the road. A van with blacked-out windows stood there, even though it was still dark outside.

"Get in," Jeffery said. "We have less than an hour until sunrise."

Jeffery walked to the driver's side and slid in, and Lucas only hesitated a second, trying to decide if he should get in the back before he slid into the passenger seat.

They drove in silence. They were further outside town than Lucas realized; the merpeople must have dragged him quite far down the river. It was twenty minutes before they passed the turnoff to where Lucas had parked to find the nymphs, but Jeffery kept driving into the city.

"How did you find me?" Lucas asked.

"There were reports of merpeople. They tend to stay hidden unless provoked, so since I was out here, I was sent to investigate."

"I didn't provoke them. I was walking down the river."

"Why?" Jeffery asked, the hurt echoing from his voice.

"I needed to clear my head. This was sudden, and I'm not dealing with it well."

"So you stole the car and started telling the rest of the magical community that the vampires killed your parents."

"They probably didn't kill my parents," Lucas relented.

"So nice of you to figure it out now and not before you made a spectacle of yourself for everyone. The nymphs are insulted that you invaded their area. They don't like men all that much."

"Especially me."

"Yes, you are the epitome of everything that they hate. A magic user not tied to nature that does not fit their narrow worldview, and you rubbed their faces in it."

"I have a feeling their worldview is going to have plenty to challenge it soon."

"What does that mean?"

"It's not my secret to tell."

Jeffery banged his hand on the steering wheel but changed the subject. "Then you go and piss off the merpeople."

"I didn't do anything to them."

"You were a vampire in their territory. You nearly started a war. I had to explain that you were young. They prize their young above all, and I had to endure a lecture from the guard about my inability to babysit. But they weren't wrong. I lost you, and you went out to this world unprepared."

"It wasn't your fault. I'm sorry. I am. I just … it is all so much. Everything happened so fast."

They drove in silence. The sun rose before they returned to the Ranch; thankfully, the protected windows kept them safe until they parked in the garage.

Jeffrey walked Lucas to his room and locked him in, leaving him alone.

The night felt long, alone in his room, without needing to sleep. Lucas hadn't even been able to stop by and pick up a new book to read. He kept the TV on most of the night, just for the company, but all that was on were old cop shows and infomercials.

By the time the door to his room began to unlock, he'd showered, changed, and was ready for a new day. He expected Jeffery to walk through, but he got Veronica instead.

She didn't seem all that happy to be seeing him either. Her face was no longer that of a seductress and instead wore the frown of a spoiled child who'd been denied something she wanted.

"I'm stuck with you," she said. "Your stunt last night got me in a lot of trouble, and if you pull anything like that again, I will tear you apart, burn you, and scatter you across the globe."

It came across as an oddly specific threat, and Lucas could not help wondering if that was how vampires were disposed of. Either that or she was trying to scare him, but he was determined not to be scared. No, he was still upset. Veronica might be acting as if she was grounded, but Lucas faced all the consequences.

"Let's go. I need to teach you all about the vampire world." She rolled her eyes as she said it, then turned and walked down the hallway, not waiting to see if he had tagged along.

Lucas only hesitated for a moment before he followed her. Veronica was not his ideal mentor, but he knew he needed to understand more about this new reality. Last night had taught him that he was extremely ignorant. The world was not what he expected, and he could no longer go off alone. He'd barely survived.

He believed Rocko that the vampires hadn't killed his parents, but he also thought that his parents left for a reason. They hadn't wanted him to be a part of this world, yet here he was, stuck in the middle.

When Veronica headed for the garage, Lucas stopped in his tracks.

"What are you waiting for?" she asked over her shoulder.

"I thought you would show me around the Ranch and maybe introduce me to the other vampires. I thought I wasn't allowed off the property for a bit."

"Did you think you were grounded?"

"I mean, yes, kind of. After last night, I expected it."

She kept walking until she went to a red sports car and slipped into the driver's seat. Not knowing what else to do, Lucas followed.

Veronica drove like nothing could harm her, even though it was still early at night and humans were on the road. She didn't let that stop her. She drove fast, swerving lanes when cars got in her way and running red lights when she could. Lucas found himself gripping tight to the seatbelt, starting to wonder if she planned to kill him and end all her problems.

"I think you should slow down," he said, feeling every minute of his forty years.

Veronica revved the engine and slipped into the wrong lane on the subdivision road, barely missing hitting an oncoming car before pulling back into the correct lane in front of the car she'd just passed.

"I can't imagine the council would approve of you drawing this much attention to yourself." Honestly, he had no idea what the council would approve of, but the werewolves seemed to like rules, and Veronica was defying all the laws of the road.

"I don't give a fuck what the council wants," she said. "I did everything I was supposed to. I filled out the paperwork, waited for permission, and they stuck me with you. Even when I proved I couldn't have known you were kin."

That last statement hit Lucas hard. The embarrassment of the council meeting still sat with him, and Veronica was only concerned with herself, as if her actions ruined her life instead of his.

"Where are we going?" Lucas asked.

Veronica didn't answer him. She just kept driving.

"I think maybe we should head back."

"Why? So, I can keep babysitting you for the next hundred years? So, your every action is tied to me for the rest of your existence? I didn't want to be a sponsor. I didn't apply for it. Instead, I begged the council to give you to anyone else." She turned, taking her eyes entirely off the road, and glared at him. "They told me that you are my responsibility, my punishment. It would be good for me to have some sniveling newborn so busy crying that he didn't realize the opportunity he'd been given." She turned back to look at the road but continued chattering nonsense about everything wrong with him.

Lucas looked down at the odometer and noticed that they were at 140 miles per hour, although they'd moved away from the residential area and were driving through the more rural areas of town. Veronica continued babbling, and Lucas became concerned that he would not walk away from this situation. If only he had enough information about vampires to know if he could withstand jumping out of the car at these speeds. He decided it was probably best not to risk it.

Suddenly, Veronica slammed on the brakes, causing the car to skid forward before stopping. They were in the middle of the road, but she didn't seem too concerned. Instead, she looked at him and spoke the first coherent words in the last few minutes. "This is all your fault. Now you need to fix it."

Lucas clicked off his seatbelt and jumped out of the car. He didn't even bother opening the door; he just sprang above it, jumping higher than he ever could have done before. Once outside, he backed away from the car, going to the side of the road, trying to give himself some distance. It didn't matter; Veronica was next to him in seconds, her eyes boring into him, mouth open, and fangs visible. He didn't think vampires could feed on each other but wasn't keen to find out.

"I don't know what you want me to do," Lucas said. "Why don't we just head back to the Ranch and talk this out?"

"Do you know how long a vampire's childhood is? At least a decade, and that is if you take to the lifestyle." Lucas stood there, letting her put her fingers on his chin and tilt his face toward her. "Do you think it is fair that I have to become someone's mother all because you are an anomaly?"

Lucas jerked away from her, shuffling back a few feet to the dirt that lined the road. Beyond this was just a field of grass. He could try and outrun her, but he knew how that had gone before. He didn't feel any better about his chances now.

"You can play the victim all you want," Lucas said. "I didn't ask to be bitten. You can hide behind your bureaucracy, but you are the one who took my blood without my consent. Then, you went on stage in front of the whole magic community and laid out my life without any sensitivity to how that would impact me. Do you have any idea how much it hurt for you to bring up the death of my parents? I still have nightmares about that night. Or the death of my mother, as if it isn't a fresh wound. Then to dead-name me, call me by that other person's name, when you decided that my body will stay like this for eternity. Do not stand there and play the victim to me. You are not my mother, and you don't have to be my sponsor. I am sure that I can find someone else to help."

"Oh yes, your boyfriend? He sure took to you quickly. It's too bad he isn't old enough; he is barely out of childhood himself. I'd pawn you off on him, but it wouldn't be more than a night before you would get in trouble again, making the whole world know what we are."

She stopped then, as if thinking through a solution to her problem.

"I screwed up," Lucas said. "I get that. No more wandering all over the magic community causing problems. I know I have a lot to learn. If you will not teach me, take me back so I can learn from someone else."

Veronica ignored him. She stood still, frozen like a statue, no longer pretending to be human. Lucas straightened, uncertain of what to do.

"If I abandon you to cause problems, I will get in trouble because you may cause mayhem in the magical community. Everyone is so worried about what would happen if the humans found out about us. The werewolves tie our hands, forcing us to no longer hunt. So, we are no longer feared. Instead, we are hidden away and used as amusement on Halloween night."

"Humans shouldn't know what we are," Lucas said. "They wouldn't be able to handle it. It would cause chaos. You have a system that works with donated blood that benefits humans as much as vampires. Why upset the balance?"

"Why?" Veronica screamed, and her whole demeanor changed to fast, jerky movements. "I have been alive for hundreds of years. Once, we hunted our prey; we collected humans as pets and let them serve us. Now we stay holed up, watching our numbers dwindle because the werewolves are too scared for us to expand. We get domesticated, no longer the monsters the world took us for. They expect me to fill out forms and babysit. All so that humans do not find out about us."

Veronica circled him, watching him as if he was still her prey.

"It seems the solution is easy."

Lucas stood tall, preparing to fight until the end to keep his existence. As screwed up as it was, it was his, and he was not going down without a fight.

But Veronica turned away from him and back toward the car. Her hand was on the door handle when she turned to him.

"I just have to teach the humans that we exist." She flashed him one of her trademark smiles, slid into the car, and peeled away before Lucas could react.

Lucas tried to run after the car. He willed his legs to pick up speed, but it'd been too long since he had fed. He was due for another feeding tonight, and it worried him that he was alone in the human world and that hunger was starting to creep up on him. Without super speed, he had nothing to do but walk back toward the Ranch. It was hard to tell the time, but the road was empty, and the sun was nowhere to be seen.

He tried to focus on finding Jeffery so that he could tell him what Veronica was up to. He hoped that the vampires would be able to stop her. But as he reached the edge of town, he didn't know where to go. There was no map of the city supernaturally imposed on his brain, and he had never been the one to drive to the Ranch. Lucas just kept walking.

As he neared the middle of town, Lucas started smelling more humans. It was later now, and most were snug safely in their houses where they were not a big temptation. However, he could hear hearts beating from a few blocks away, ones that were excited, and he found his feet taking him toward the thrumming.

When he got closer, he started to recognize the area. This was his part of town. He passed his apartment without pause and continued until he reached the city's downtown area. A few restaurants were open that still had customers, and he was tempted to go in and find himself a meal, but the stench of the food mixed in with the blood minimized the appeal. He followed his instinct toward a more familiar area, his hunting ground.

Lucas had never hunted before; it felt like there were two sides of himself: the side battling with him, telling him that this was not what he wanted and not where he should go. Then there was the other side, the hungry side. It was more primal and basic, and all it wanted was blood.

When Lucas opened the door to Rocko's, he was a shell of himself, guided mainly by an instinct that'd been hardwired into his vampire genetic code. He glanced over the bar, taking stock of the room. It was about half full, and most clientele tonight were human. Lucas scanned the room carefully and found his target. A man was drinking at the bar. He was cute enough, but most importantly, he was alone and vulnerable. Lucas's fangs dropped at the thought of a meal, and he had to concentrate to make them disappear. Humans couldn't see that. They couldn't find out about vampires.

A distant part of his brain grasped on to this thought. Then he remembered Veronica. He remembered the betrayal of being fed on without permission. Lucas focused on the hurt and anger and used the emotions to ignore the pull toward the single drunk man.

He walked, with his fists clenched, up to Mika.

"I need to talk to you," he said. "Upstairs."

Then, without speaking again, without pulling in any more of the delicious human scent, he walked past the stunned barkeep and straight up to Rocko's room.

It was easier there, even though he could hear all the humans below. Lucas started humming to their heartbeats, but that required him to breathe, so he began to pace instead. He was fidgety by the time the witch and Rocko made it upstairs, even though it had been seconds.

"Why are you alone?" Rocko asked.

"Veronica," Lucas managed to say. His fangs were out now, and he felt as if it was taking all his control not to go downstairs and sink them into the first human he found. Thankfully, the witch did not tempt him enough, and Lucas was reasonably sure that Rocko was strong enough to stop him if he lost control.

"Yes, Veronica is supposed to be your sponsor. Why isn't she with you? How did you end up back here?" the witch said. There was anger in her voice, and Lucas focused on that to help him pay attention to the words he needed to say.

"Veronica drove me away. She wasn't happy that I was put in her charge. So she decided to tell the humans about vampires. She wanted to go hunting."

"She has been going on about that for years," Rocko said. "All the old ones do occasionally, but they know better. The new system has too many benefits."

"She meant it. She left me to walk back. She plans on making vampires come out so that she doesn't have me for the next decade. I think that idea broke what common sense she had. I thought she planned to hunt, but maybe the plan was leaving me, knowing I would get hungry and not be able to control it."

Lucas slunk to the ground, his knees pulled up to his chest, and his hands tugging on his hair as if hoping he could cause some other pain to distract himself from the hunger that had captured him.

"Call the Ranch," Rocko said.

"Jeffery," Lucas said.

The witch pulled out a cell phone and called. Lucas heard her ask for Jeffery and tell him what had happened. He even heard Jeffery cursing on the other side of the line. Vampire hearing was amazing.

Rocko reached down and picked up Lucas, putting him in his bed on top of the untouched bedspread. He sat beside them both in a gesture that seemed protective, as if he were defending his patrons below.

"I don't want the whole horde in my bar," Rocko said.

"I won't harm anyone," Lucas said. "I don't want to hunt. I can go down through the backdoor."

"That's a good idea. Tell Jeffery to meet us outside and tell the rest of the horde to meet at the hall. We need to convene tonight. Veronica may have a bigger plan, and we at least need to make sure everyone is warned."

Rocko picked up Lucas again, holding him securely as he maneuvered him out the backdoor and into the alley. Mika had stayed behind at the bar, so it was just the two of them as they walked away, waiting for Jeffery to meet them.

"Sorry I brought trouble to your place," Lucas said.

"I think you might just *be* trouble. As long as you can hold your fangs, you are welcome. You are family now, even more than before. Although, next time, don't come hungry."

Lucas managed a chuckle as he heard a car pull up. The passenger window rolled down, showing Jeffery in the driver's seat.

"How is he doing?" Jeffery asked.

"I've been better," Lucas said.

Rocko helped Lucas in the passenger seat, delicately, at odds with the nearly indestructible being that he'd become.

Jeffery saw him, cursed again, and then took off as soon as the car door closed.

"You were scheduled for a feeding tonight. When you didn't show, they thought you ran off again."

"Slow down," Lucas said, trying to sound more in control than he was. The pain had lessened some as they moved away from the humans. "Veronica took me out of the Ranch. I went because I wasn't sure what else to do. I didn't know how angry she was. She left me outside of town. Veronica plans on revealing vampires to the humans."

Jeffery swore again and hit his hand on the steering wheel, causing it to bounce enough that Lucas was worried it would break.

"I knew they shouldn't have left you with her. That explains why everyone is going to the town hall. She didn't have a lot of faith in you to handle yourself."

"It helps that I know there is another way. I didn't grow up like her, learning that preying on humans was how to survive."

"No, but don't try to excuse her either. Many older vampires have adjusted. Most prefer it. They have watched too many of our kind be hunted and killed. They have seen too many humans accidentally killed."

Jeffery parked in the garage and moved to the passenger door, helping Lucas out. The hunger had taken over and it took Jeffery guiding him to make it down to the lab.

"The stray is back." It was the same doctor as before.

"Veronica snatched him and left him out in the country. He found himself at Rocko's, but he got away clean. Now the hunger has him."

"Impressive for a newbie."

They led him back into a private room; Jeffery followed without comment from Lucas or the doctor. Lucas's fangs were out, and while the desire had lessened as they'd moved away from the humans, he was still overwhelmed with pain and longing. It ate at him, and when the doctor brought in the warmed blood, he didn't even think twice before he drank the entire cup and then looked down, as if hopeful for more.

"Your body needs to settle. If you drink everything now, you risk going into a frenzy. They will bring back more soon," Jeffery said.

"You can have more in ten minutes." They left a digital timer on the table, and Lucas stared at it intensely, focusing on nothing else but the numbers counting down. When it reached zero, he stood up to demand more blood, but the doctor was there with another cup.

He drank this one slower, but it was still gone too quickly.

The doctor set the timer for ten more minutes. It was easier to wait this time, but his stomach still demanded more.

When the third cup came, it was harder to start sipping from it, but he managed to get it all down. The doctor looked at him expectantly with the timer in their hand, but he waved it away.

"I think I'm done."

They nodded as if satisfied and turned to walk away.

"How often am I supposed to feed?" Lucas asked.

The doctor looked at him in surprise.

"Veronica is his sponsor," Jeffery said.

With a sigh, the doctor came back to the curtained area.

"How often you need to feed depends. Most older vampires are here nightly. Newer vampires go longer. You should have been here tonight before the frenzy overtook you. You won't need as much if you feed regularly."

"Veronica could run fast, but I tried and couldn't do it. I had to walk into town. I didn't get tired, but is something wrong with me?"

"No, the main part of the transition takes three days. At that point, you are more vampire than human, but parts of yourself are still transitioning over. As of tonight, you are now completely vampire."

"Wait, does that mean I could have changed myself while still part human?"

"No, we would have told you if something could have been done," Jeffery said.

Lucas nodded and turned away from the empty cup in disgust. Blood smelled horrible when you weren't hungry.

"The council leader wanted me to tell you two to go to the town hall when he was cleared. I think they need him to give testimony."

"Am I safe to go?"

"You are fed, and your restraint tonight was admirable. Jeffery will make sure you don't get into any more trouble."

Lucas looked up at Jeffery with a smile and reached out to take his hand. "Thanks for saving me. Again."

"At least this time, you weren't making bad decisions."

"I guess vampires can at least learn new tricks."

Lucas sat in the car, his hand on the door handle, unable to force himself to open it. Jeffery sat patiently in the driver's seat, giving Lucas space.

"It won't be like last time," Jeffery said.

"You don't know that."

"I do. For one, Veronica isn't going to be there. She was the problem."

Lucas knew he needed to go into the meeting to tell them precisely what was happening. The situation was severe, and he was concerned that humans could get hurt. However, no amount of rational thinking was helping his anxiety.

"Let's go," said Lucas.

"You're ready?"

"No, I don't think I will ever be ready, but it has to be done."

As they approached the building, they could hear a lot of loud voices and even some yelling. When they opened the door and stepped in, the room silenced, and everyone turned to look at the two men.

"Here he is," Elizabeth, the vampire leader said. She gestured for him to move forward, and Lucas felt Jeffery's hand on his shoulder, pressing him to proceed.

"It's about time," an older man said from a council seat. Lucas recognized him from the last time. He looked human, but he knew better now. He had to be a witch.

"Now, Robert," the vampire council member said. "You wouldn't want us to bring a hungry vampire out in public, would you? He showed restraint, but if we hadn't fed him first, it would just be asking for trouble. He's a baby, after all."

Lucas was figuring out that the terminology used to describe new vampires probably contributed to Veronica snapping. They kept talking about him as if he was incapable of anything instead of needing guidance in a new world. No wonder Veronica had become angry at the idea of being tied to him.

"Before we ask the vampire to continue with his testimony, the council would like first to apologize." It was the werewolf alpha who spoke. "While the information that Veronica gave during the last council session was important in understanding what caused you to turn, it should not have been allowed to be delivered in such a way. It was not until her conclusion that I realized incorrect pronouns and names were being used. I want you to know that the records have been corrected and that the council will not tolerate any bigotry moving forward. The magical community has received enough hate that we should all have acceptance and understanding."

This last line was said to the room at large, and it was easy for Lucas to pick up on the not-so-subtle hint that not everyone was as tolerant and accepting as the werewolf wanted them to be. But he would take the apology, which rarely happened, especially that sincerely.

"Thank you," Lucas said. He was aware now that everyone in the room was focused on him.

"Now, why don't you explain to the council why we were called."

"As you know," Lucas said, "the council made Veronica my sponsor. Tonight, when the sun went down, she took me off of the Ranch. She was driving very fast, and I was concerned that humans might realize it wasn't natural. She stopped outside of town and became frustrated. She seemed to latch on to the idea of humans finding out about vampires and decided it was a good thing instead of a bad one. She went on about how she missed the good old days when vampires could hunt."

"I got dragged out of bed for this?" Robert, the witch, said.

"She left me alone outside of town. It took all my control not to attack a human, but I don't think that was her goal. She is so focused on not wanting to be my sponsor that she seemed willing to go to all sorts of extremes."

"Elizabeth, what do you have to say?"

The vampire council member spoke up. "Most of the old ones have lamented about the past, but we know that the new rules keep us alive. There have been concerns. That is why Veronica was granted a pass. She needed a hunt to move forward. It is possible that the responsibility from that hunt became too much, and she is in a frenzy."

There was a gasp from the room, and Lucas looked at Jeffery with concern. A frenzy was what they used to describe him earlier in the evening. It was terrible, but he managed to survive without hurting anyone. Maybe Veronica would come to her senses, and Lucas had worried everyone for nothing.

"A frenzy in one so old?" Robert said. There was fear tracing his voice.

"Do we know where she has gone?" another council member asked.

The room turned and looked at Lucas again. "Um, no. She drove off. She was headed out of town."

"Which way?" someone asked. There was so much happening in the room that Lucas couldn't tell who was speaking.

"We were on the west side of town, I think, by the fields. She drove away from there but was gone so fast that I don't know where she ended up."

"I think it is safe to assume that she headed into the city," Elizabeth said.

"Wouldn't that be good?" Lucas asked Jeffery. "At least in the city, she wouldn't be noticed."

"In the city," Elizabeth said, "there are more people to see. If she wanted a spectacle, then that is where she would need to go."

The council members started talking over each other, followed by people in the audience. It was a loud mess, and Lucas noticed the same female wolf huddled in the corner with her hands pressing a pair of headphones to her ears as if to block out the noise.

"Enough," the alpha wolf said. "We have heard testimony and found that the vampires cannot handle their own. It is up to the council to control this situation."

"It was the council that caused this situation in the first place," Elizabeth said. "If you had just listened to me, a different situation could have happened, but you insist on treating us all as wolves. We do not require the same handling as your pups. We agreed to this council for the sake of peace, but we find that it is now hampering that very peace. Maybe it is time that we rethink our participation here."

"That is the first smart thing the vampires have observed," Robert said. "We have our own rich history, and you would superimpose your ideas onto others."

He looked at Lucas when he said this, and even though Elizabeth and Robert seemed to be stating the same thing, Lucas thought they meant it differently.

"This council is here to bring order, to keep the town of Ember safe," the werewolf said. "The council has saved us from tearing each other apart."

"The council was never intended to be under your ultimate control," Elizabeth said. She stood in her seat and stepped out onto the table. Her movement was swift and coordinated without any of the awkwardness of youth. She jumped from the table directly to the council room floor in one fluid motion. As she walked out, the other vampires followed her. When Jeffery started to move, Lucas took one last look at the room and followed. For better or worse, they were his people now, and he knew he needed to go with them.

Neither talked until they reached their car and were driving back toward the Ranch.

"That can't have been good," Lucas said.

"The council has been the foundation of Ember for nearly three hundred years. But there has been tension. The council members are supposed to change out every decade, but the werewolf alpha is six months overdue. Your creation and Veronica's crusade were just the tipping point for everything."

"What happens next?"

"We let the grownups work everything out and hope we don't get drafted into a war. Every so often, the older vampires will talk about the last one that ended up in the council's creation."

When they returned to the Ranch, it was livelier than usual. The previously vacant halls were brimming with movement. It appeared everyone had already been called back to the main house. There was an eagerness in the air, as if they'd been sleepwalking before but had now been brought back to life. Lucas couldn't help the chill that ran down his spine at the thought that the vampires were happy at an impending war and that he was now part of their family. If Jeffery hadn't been by his side, he wasn't sure he could have walked through the house and back up to his room. He was even more glad when Jeffery went in with him.

"It's not the violence that they are excited about," Jeffery said, as if reading his mind. "It is the change of pace. Things tend to be the same, and when there is something different, it causes them to be excited. They don't want a war; they want a diversion, and Veronica has given them that."

"Do they want her to out them to the humans? It would give them quite a diversion."

"I'm too young to remember when they hunted, but I have heard stories, and many vampires didn't make it. Humans might be scared of monsters, but when they are scared, they attack with everything they have. This isn't going to happen in one night. Veronica must devise a way to survive before she follows through on her plans."

Jeffery moved closer to Lucas, their lips touched, and their hands wrapped around each other.

When night came again, they were still naked and sprawled out on the bed. Neither expected the bedroom door to fly open and a man to walk in. Lucas only saw the vague outline of his long brown hair, thick beard, and sun-kissed skin before Lucas reached for a blanket to cover himself. He shot up and headed to the bathroom before the unknown man saw his naked body, but a set of hands reached out and stopped him before he could escape.

"You're mine. I don't have time to coddle you and teach you everything you should already know. You don't have anything I haven't seen. Now get some clothes on."

Lucas wanted to shower. He wanted privacy. Instead, he got some grizzly vampire who had to be at least a century old watching him as he threw on his jeans and the first shirt he saw. It was Jeffery's, and it fit him tighter than he liked. The outline of his binder was visible through the thin material.

"Are you coming or staying?" the vampire asked Jeffery.

"Coming," Jeffery said, and Lucas felt instant relief.

The older vampire turned from Jeffery and focused on Lucas. "I'm Joseph—you can call me Joe—and I'm your new sponsor. I haven't had an infant in many years, and I don't plan on having you for very long. I'll tell you what you need to know. If you have questions, you come to me. If you need to leave the Ranch, don't. You are now on restrictions for the foreseeable future. And that goes for everyone without permission of the vampire council. So don't go complaining to me."

Joe took them on a tour of the mansion. They walked fast, with the older man rapidly pointing out the common areas and introducing him to every vampire they encountered. Every available space was full. There were too many names for Lucas to remember.

Lucas noticed that every time a new vampire was introduced, Joe switched pronouns without stopping to think. People were smashed together from so many different cultures and periods that the whole concept of what was considered feminine and masculine fluctuated from one person to another. Lucas realized that gender was accepted without question in the vampire community. There were she's, he's, they's, and more pronouns that Lucas heard for the first time. The introductions were made without any awkwardness, but they were fast.

Sexuality also seemed to be accepted. Jeffery was allowed on the tour, so it was automatically assumed that they were important to each other. Despite his relationship with Jeffery, Lucas had assumed that vampires were solo creatures. He soon found out how wrong he was. Just as many vampires were introduced as families as those who were not. The groups varied from platonic partnerships to couples and polyamorous relationships. The information was provided as a matter of fact in the introductions.

No one questioned Lucas's identity or paid any attention when Jeffery reached for Lucas's hand to lend support. By the time they walked through the estate, even with the buzz of uncertainty, Lucas was as happy as he'd ever been. Maybe it wasn't the life he would have chosen or the body he would have preferred for eternity, but for the first time, he felt at home. He couldn't help but feel a sting of resentment toward Veronica. If she'd taken the time to show him this world, then the adjustment would not have been as hard.

When the tour ended, Joe left them, telling them he had prepa-
rations to make and that he expected Jeffery to keep Lucas out of
trouble. Eventually, the pair settled in the library with a group of
other newer vampires who were all trying to stay out of the way.
They sat in silence, waiting to find out what would happen next.

The entire Ranch was on alert as soon as she reached the gate. Lucas watched the security camera over Joseph's shoulder. She had no car and easily ducked under the bar which stopped vehicles from entering. There wasn't much in the way of security, but it was a warning before a mob came. The vampires could handle their own.

Lucas recognized her. She was the quiet werewolf girl from the meeting, the one who wore headphones over her ears. She was either brave or stupid for walking into enemy territory alone. From the look of her face in the grainy black-and-white footage from the security cameras that tracked her, she wasn't sure which one she was either.

"What's the alpha's daughter doing here?" one of the vampires asked. Lucas tried to remember his name; *Andre or Andrew*, he thought. With his billowy shirts and leather pants, he looked like a pirate.

When she knocked on the door, the vampires all moved to the entryway. The more senior vampires were in front, with Elizabeth opening the door. Lucas was up on the railing, trying to see through some taller vampires blocking his way. Thankfully, he found he could hear perfectly.

"I'm sorry for not calling before I came," the werewolf said. "I appreciate you allowing me to speak before you attack."

She stood tall, facing straight ahead, her face nearly blank of all emotions, but her hands at her sides conveyed her nerves. Her fingers were twisting as if in some weird dance.

Lucas looked at Jeffery, hoping that he would provide some insight. However, anything they said would be heard, so he turned his attention back to the conversation below.

"Does the alpha know that you are here?" Elizabeth asked.

Looking down, the size difference between Elizabeth and the werewolf was overwhelming. The girl hadn't looked that big standing next to others of her kind, but here among the vampires who had once just been human, she was both tall and muscular.

"No," she said. Then, she seemed to gain confidence and continued, "My father, the alpha, does not know I am here. However, as the heir to the pack, I have a right to handle pack negotiations."

"And what do you hope to negotiate?"

"I understand your frustration. The pack is too inflexible and has been enforcing our own rules onto other cultures. That is not how the council should work. It should be a cohesion where no one's voice is greater than the others. My father should have stepped down as the head of the council, and it should be the vampires' turn. We all know that. He hasn't because he is worried about his pack."

"He is worried that his only offspring is a female who will not mate and is abnormal."

"I'm not abnormal," the words tore through her in a growl. "I am autistic and asexual, and there is nothing wrong with either one. It doesn't stop me from leading the pack. My lack of a mate and offspring is not an issue either. I will adopt an heir. It has been done before for many reasons."

"Yes, it has, and from what I have heard, your father plans on doing so himself."

"I am my father's heir. All I need is your assistance."

"You want us to overthrow the alpha and put you in charge? It would be safer for the town if we went to war now."

"I am not overthrowing anyone. I need time. For that, I need you to take no action against the pack. We will help in whatever way we can with Veronica, and I will work to get you, or whomever you designate, as the head of the council for the next term."

"You can do this?"

"I can." She stood as if at military attention, trying to convey her strength. "Just give me a week before you move."

"How do we know this isn't a trick?"

"You know my father, you know my pack. You know what I say is true."

Lucas was impressed with her determination. It had to take a lot to stand up and let herself be judged by someone who might just as well be her enemy, when she was having difficulty within her own family. The tension in the room was strong, and he knew that everything hinged on these next words. If Elizabeth disagreed, this young lady might not return to her people alive.

Elizabeth bowed her head. "One week, pup. You have one week to show your father you are an alpha. After that, we will do what we need to keep this town and the world safe from one of ours."

The werewolf just turned, showing her back to the vampires, as if testing their word, and walked out the front door. Lucas was one of the closest to the security room, and he and Jeffery were the only ones who returned to watch the werewolf.

The girl collapsed on the ground, rocking back and forth as if the meeting had taken all of her strength. After less than a minute, she pulled herself up and continued out of vampire territory.

WHAT TO READ NEXT

Continue the Ember Town Series

Phoenix

ACKNOWLEDGMENTS

As I sit here about to send my fourth book and my first series out into the world, I am overwhelmed again by the community I have found. A huge thank you to everyone who has read my books. You have seen a part of my soul and came back for more. Thank you to everyone who follows me on social media, who likes my posts, and forwards them on. People continue to find me because of you.

I want to give a huge thank you to the writing community that I have found. Being an independently published author is not so lonely when you have so many taking the journey with you. Thank you for letting me read your books and be a part of your journey. Thank you for being part of mine.

A special thanks to my team. A huge thank you to the NeuroSpicy writing group who is always there to bounce ideas and provide feedback. To my beta readers, who took the time to provide me with early feedback. Specifically, thank you to Elizabeth and Lilian. I am so excited to be working with a new editor, Rebecca, on this project. May this series be the first of many collaborations. I am extremely grateful to have Skye Alley working again to proofread and narrate my stories so they can reach more readers.

As always, I am extremely grateful to my youngest kid, who hears more about my books than they could possibly want, yet they still keep listening, to my son, who is always a phone call away to discuss or debate any issue, and to my daughter.